Murder with a Touch of Spice

A Spice Sisters Mystery

Gloria Hander Lyons

Blue Sage Press

Murder with a Touch of Spice
A Spice Sisters Mystery

Copyright © 2013 by Gloria Hander Lyons

Inquires should be addressed to:
Blue Sage Press
www.BlueSagePress.com

ISBN: 978-0-9842438-4-6

Library of Congress Control Number: 2013913357

First Edition: August 2013

Printed in the United States of America

This book is dedicated to
Tom Rizzo and Larry Watts,
my writing partners in crime.

You not only inspired me to dust off that
novel languishing in the bottom of my
desk drawer and get it into print,
you used your valuable time and expertise
to help edit the manuscript.

Thanks for your inspiration,
encouragement and friendship.

I couldn't have done it without your help!

* * * * * *

Thanks also to Coral Beach and
Carolyn Watts, whose "eagle eyes"
helped spot many of those pesky typos.

Other Books by Gloria Hander Lyons

- Easy Microwave Desserts in a Mug
- Easy Microwave Desserts in a Mug for Kids
- Just Fun Decorating for Tweens & Teens
- Decorating Basics: For Men Only
- Ten Common Home Decorating Mistakes & How to Avoid Them
- If Teapots Could Talk—Fun Ideas for Tea Parties
- Lavender Sensations: Fragrant Herbs for Home & Bath
- A Taste of Lavender: Delectable Treats with an Exotic Floral Flavor
- Self-Publishing on a Budget: A Do-It-All-Yourself Guide
- Kiss My Grits, Sugar: Southern Humor with a Side of Tasty Fixin's
- The Secret Ingredient: Tasty Recipes with an Unusual Twist
- Hand Over the Chocolate & No One Gets Hurt: The Chocolate-Lover's Cookbook
- Flamingos, Poodle Skirts & Red Hots: Creative Theme Party Ideas
- Quick Gifts From the Kitchen: No Cooking Required
- 40 Favorite Impossible Pies: Main Dishes & Desserts
- Quick & Easy Sandwich Wraps
- A Taste of Memories: Comforting Foods From Our Past
- Pearls of Wisdom for Creating a Joyful Life
- What's Up with That? Humorous Short Stories About Life in Modern-Day America

For a complete list of books written by Gloria Hander Lyons,
visit her websites at: www.GloriaHanderLyons.com
and www.BlueSagePress.com

Chapter One

Ginger knew she shouldn't have gone to The Grand Hotel that morning. Her intuition kept telling her not to go, but she had an appointment to view a wedding reception site in the Bluebonnet Ballroom on the second floor with one of her brides. As a top-notch professional wedding planner, she couldn't let her client down. Finally, her sense of duty won out.

The next thing she knew, she was tumbling down a flight of marble stairs along with Maybelle Jamison, in a tangled mass of flailing arms and legs, landing at the bottom on the highly polished granite floor. Then the whole world went black.

When Ginger opened her eyes, she found herself in the emergency room with her left arm in a cast, her painfully sore ribs tightly bandaged and the Morgan County Sheriff lurking outside the door.

* * * * * * * * * *

Nurse Evelyn Crane woke up that morning with the same nagging premonition. "Don't go! Don't go!" But then, she had that same feeling every workday morning—she worked in the emergency room at Mercy Hospital. There are a lot of crazy people out there, and eventually they all turn up in the ER. It was fate, or maybe it was just her bad karma. She knew the minute the staircase victims arrived—one unconscious and banged up, the other one dead—this day was going downhill in a hurry.

Just as she started to process the surviving patient's paperwork, the family members began to arrive.

"I'm looking for my wife," said a tall, out-of-breath, fifty-something gentleman, running up to the nursing station.

"And you are?"

"Mace," he replied between gulps of air. "Mace McCormick. My wife, Ginger, was brought in by an ambulance this morning."

"Dad!" screamed two attractive, identical young women, as they entered the ER doors.

"Pepper, Curry," he cried, hugging them both.

Lord have mercy, thought Nurse Crane, shaking her head and crossing her chubby brown arms over her ample belly. It looks like we're starting this day off with a spice rack. We've got a Ginger, a Mace, a Pepper and a Curry.

Peering over the tops of her narrow reading glasses at the spice trio, she informed them, "Ginger McCormick is in exam room number four with Dr. Martin. But only one of you can go in at a time," she warned.

"I'll be back as soon as I find out how she is," Mace told his daughters, racing down the hallway toward the examination rooms.

The twin sisters turned to Nurse Crane.

"Is she all right?" asked Curry.

"Is she conscious?" asked Pepper.

But before the nurse could get a single word out, she heard more screams, "Pepper, Curry!"

Pepper and Curry spun around when they heard their sisters' voices.

"Cinnamon, Sage," they cried in unison. And once again the group was in a hugfest.

"Lord save me," exclaimed the nurse. "I'll never look at spices the same way again."

"We're here to see Ginger McCormick," said Sage. "Is she okay?"

"I just have one question," said Nurse Crane. "Are there any more of you spices I need to know about?"

The four sisters rolled their eyes, annoyed by her comment.

"No," quipped Sage, weary from a lifetime of spice jokes. "We're all here."

"Hallelujah," mumbled Nurse Crane, glancing heavenward. "Your mother is fine. By some miracle, her only injuries are a broken left wrist, a couple of cracked ribs and a mild concussion."

"Oh, thank God," said Cinnamon.

"Dad is with her now," added Pepper.

Sage glanced down the hallway toward the examination rooms and locked eyes with her long-time nemesis, Sheriff Jason Winters. Jason and Sage grew up in the same small town of Clearwater, Texas, where both their parents still lived. Years later, they landed in nearby Houston, starting their careers in law.

Jason, a police officer, worked his way up through the ranks to the level of detective in record time. Sage was a criminal trial lawyer, whose defense of a few questionable wealthy clients caused her to butt heads with the cocky Detective Winters on more than one occasion.

Jason later left the Houston Police Department and ran for the office of Sheriff in Morgan County, which included Clearwater. Jason and Sage were like two super-charged lightning bolts, drawn to each other but unable to occupy the same space at the same time without generating a shower of electric sparks.

Sage marched up to Jason, her short auburn curls bouncing with each determined step, "What are you doing here?"

"Murder investigation," he replied, admiring the way her dark blue suit hugged the curves of her short but shapely figure.

"Murder? What are you talking about?"

"Maybelle Jamison was stabbed with a knife before she went tumbling down the stairs with Ginger."

"Maybelle was stabbed? But why? Was it robbery?"

"Nothing was stolen," said Jason. "But Ginger was the last person to see the victim alive, so I need to get her statement."

"You think my mother killed Maybelle?" asked an outraged Sage, her cheeks beginning to flush with anger.

Jason frowned. "It's part of any routine investigation. You know that."

Sage narrowed her eyes, "She's not talking to anyone without a lawyer present."

"That's fine with me, Counselor."

When Dr. Martin left the exam room, he nodded his approval for Sage and Jason to enter.

"Mother, are you okay?" asked Sage, gently planting a kiss on her mother's forehead, the only spot left on Ginger's body without a bruise, scrape or bandage.

"Hello, Jason," said Mace, stepping forward to greet the young man with a hand-shake.

"Good to see you, Mace," replied Jason. He turned toward Ginger, wincing at the sight of her injuries. How had she managed to survive such a fall? She was lucky to be alive.

"I know you must be in a lot of pain right now," he told her, "and I'm really sorry to bother you, but I need to ask a few questions about your accident. We now know that Maybelle Jamison was stabbed before she fell down the stairs, and since you were the last person to see her before she died, I need to take your statement about what happened there this morning."

"Are you saying Maybelle was murdered?" asked Ginger in disbelief, glancing over at Mace.

Mace lowered his head sadly and closed his eyes. Maybelle was Mace's first wife. They had been married only two years before she realized that Mace, an aeronautical engineer for a NASA contractor, wasn't meeting her economic and social expectations. She left him for a wealthy real estate developer with lofty political aspirations. Maybelle was quite a handful, and Mace wasn't sorry when she left, but he certainly never wished her any harm.

"Yes," replied Jason. "We think she was stabbed in one of the meeting rooms on the second floor, but managed to walk to the main staircase before she collapsed and fell down the stairs."

"Oh, my word," said Ginger. "I didn't see anyone else near the stairs when I got there. About halfway down, I heard a noise behind me and turned around just in time to see Maybelle tumbling down the stairs. She crashed into me, and then we both rolled down to the bottom of the staircase. I blacked out after that."

"We haven't found the murder weapon yet," added Jason, "but the autopsy showed a stab wound to the abdomen. We believe it was a serrated knife—like a steak knife. You didn't see anyone else on the second floor before you reached the stairs?"

"Just my bridal client and the hotel event coordinator, Jenny Hall, who was showing us the ballroom. But Jenny left about ten o'clock for another meeting on the second floor, and I stayed to discuss a few more wedding details with the bride. After she left, I packed up my briefcase and headed for the stairs."

"Okay then," said Jason, jotting a few notes in his notebook before replacing it in his shirt pocket. "I appreciate your time, Ginger. If you think of anything else that might help us with this case, just call me."

Sage bristled noticeably; glaring at him.

"Or have your lawyer call me," he revised, with a quick glance in Sage's direction.

Jason left the room, with Sage following close behind like a testy little terrier nipping at his heels. Ginger and Mace looked at each other knowingly.

"The dance of romance," said Mace. "Those two have been at it for years."

"Do you think they will ever let their guards down long enough to figure out what all that tension is really about?" asked Ginger.

"I hope so. They could be a dynamic duo—just like us," replied Mace, giving Ginger's uninjured hand a loving squeeze.

Sage trailed Jason down the hallway, her low-heeled lawyer pumps working double-time to keep up with his long strides. "Do you have any suspects for this murder—other than my mother?"

Jason turned to face her. Those electric green eyes and sensuous lips always made his insides quiver. But why was she always so cantankerous whenever he was around? He never deliberately tried to piss her off. He had set his sights on this feisty little fireball a long time ago, but it was taking a bit longer than anticipated to rein her in. He felt confident, though, that she would come around eventually. Jason was a patient man.

"Once again, Counselor, in case you missed it the first time, I'm just doing my job. I can't ignore the fact that your mother was the last one to see the victim alive, not to mention the fact that they were acquaintances and possibly even rivals."

"That's ridiculous," countered Sage, planting her hands firmly on both hips. "Maybelle left my father long before he met my mother."

Jason shrugged his broad shoulders and turned to leave. There was no point in arguing over this issue. It wasn't going to change the way he approached the investigation.

Sage fumed as she watched him walk away. Why did God have to waste that tall, dark and sexy body on such a stubborn, narrow-minded man? Every time she saw him, she bristled and went weak in the knees at the same time. Why did he always affect her that way?

Never mind, she'd have to think about that another day. She and her sisters had their work cut out for them. They needed to find out who killed Maybelle Jamison.

* * * * * * * * * *

"Murder?" exclaimed Cinnamon, when Sage told her sisters about the stabbing.

"Why would anyone want to murder Maybelle?" asked Pepper.

"That's what we have to find out," replied Sage, "before Jason throws Mother in jail!"

"He doesn't really believe Mother killed Maybelle, does he?" asked Curry.

"Probably not," admitted Sage. "But Mother was the last person to see Maybelle alive, so he has to treat her like any other suspect until he proves otherwise."

"Or until we prove otherwise," declared Cinnamon.

"Exactly," confirmed Sage.

"Where do we start?" asked Pepper.

"We need to find out why Maybelle was at the hotel this morning," replied Sage. "I know her daughter, Cynthia. Maybe she can help."

"The killer could have stolen a steak knife from the hotel kitchen," added Cinnamon. "I could snoop around in there. Gordon, the hotel chef, was one of my instructors at culinary school."

Cinnamon was a professional chef. After working at several well-known restaurants around the country, she formed a partnership with two other students in her culinary class to start their own restaurant in the trendy Galleria area of Houston. At 29, her talent and hard work had put her on the path to a successful entrepreneurial career, which didn't leave much time for a social life.

"Curry and I could question some of the hotel employees," offered Pepper, "to see if they saw anything suspicious."

"It's a start," agreed Sage. "Let's get on it. Call me as soon as you have any leads."

The sisters scattered in different directions, hot on the trail of Maybelle's killer. Sage pulled out her cell phone and searched for Cynthia Jamison's number. Cynthia and Sage, both 32, were married to their demanding careers. They attended the same law school, starting off as competitive rivals and ending up as close friends, both returning to Houston to practice law at competing firms.

After getting a voice mail message on Cynthia's cell phone, Sage tried her office number, and finally tracked her down at Maybelle's house. She should have known the family would gather there in the wake of such unexpected tragedy.

"Cynthia, this is Sage McCormick. I'm so sorry to hear about your mother's death."

"Thank you, Sage. I heard your mother is in the hospital. Is she going to be all right?"

"Yes, she should be fine, but the Sheriff was at the hospital and told us Maybelle was murdered."

"It's horrible," Cynthia sobbed. "I just don't understand why someone would want to kill Mother."

"I can't believe it either," replied Sage. "Jason took my mother's statement about the incident as part of the investigation, but I want to do some investigating on my own. Could I stop by and talk with you for a few minutes today?"

"I don't know what you expect to find out by talking to me, but I'll do anything I can to help. I want that killer caught, too. Come over to the house around one o'clock and we'll see what we can figure out."

"Thank you," said Sage. It was almost noon, so she dashed off to grab a sandwich at Anton's Deli, her favorite lunch spot in Clearwater. Whenever Sage was stressed, she automatically thought of food. It worked better than tranquilizers to calm her nerves, and the thought of one of Anton's hot grilled chicken Panini sandwiches with sautéed red peppers and a thick layer of melted cheese made her mouth water.

She scarfed down her sandwich, topped it off with a delectable, fudgey brownie and felt fully charged and ready to tackle the world. Next, she checked in with her secretary to make sure there were no pending crises at the office, and headed over to the local library to do a bit of research on Maybelle Jamison.

After leaving Mace, Maybelle married a wealthy real estate developer named Henry Jamison. He was one of many developers who capitalized on the Gulf Coast location of Clearwater and turned it into an upscale tourist attraction with million-dollar waterfront homes, expensive seafood restaurants, huge marinas, and retail/entertainment complexes. Even though Clearwater was a small town, with a population of only 22,000, the millions of tourists it attracted each year fostered a booming economy.

Maybelle thrived on social status and wealth. As Sage scanned the social columns in the local newspaper, she noticed that Maybelle was the star attraction for most of the social and charity events. Her husband was elected Mayor of Clearwater, and then moved on up the political ladder to the office of U. S. Representative. But somewhere along the way, Maybelle made a dangerous enemy.

* * * * * * * * * *

While Sage gathered information about Maybelle's social status, Cinnamon called her former instructor, Gordon Ellis, head chef at The Grand Hotel. She explained the situation her mother was in because of Maybelle's untimely demise, and asked if he could help her with a little investigating.

"Of course, Cinnamon. I'll do whatever I can to help," he replied. "But the deputies have already searched this hotel from top to bottom looking for the murder weapon, and they came up empty handed."

"I just want to check things out for myself," explained Cinnamon. "My mother is on the Sheriff's murder suspect list, and I need to do everything I can to get her off."

The Grand Hotel, built as a palatial residence for a ship-building magnate in 1925, overlooks Pelican Bay, a tiny inlet on the Gulf of Mexico. Well-known business developer, Clinton Tate, purchased the building a few years ago and turned it into an elegant hotel with a five-star restaurant on the first floor, spacious ballrooms and meeting rooms on the second floor, and luxurious guest rooms on the third floor. The beautiful, sweeping marble staircase in the entry is a favorite photo spot for brides.

Cinnamon planned to arrive at the hotel close to noon, during the lunch time rush, so she could snoop around without being watched too carefully—not an easy feat for a woman who's two inches shy of six feet tall, with short, spiky, reddish-blonde hair. And like her mother and three sisters, she was blessed (or sometimes cursed) with a dogged determination. Just like bloodhounds, when they latched onto a scent, they refused to give up until they caught their prey. The hunt was on!

"The Sheriff said the murder weapon might have been a steak knife," Cinnamon told Gordon. "Is there any way to tell if one of your knives is missing?"

"Unfortunately not," he replied. "We have hundreds of steak knives."

"Did you see Maybelle at the hotel this morning?"

"No, I was in a meeting with Jenny Hall at ten o'clock, and I didn't see Maybelle until after the accident. Jenny and I heard screams in the lobby and ran out to see what was going on. That's when we saw Maybelle and Ginger at the bottom of the stairs."

"Do you have any idea why Maybelle was here at the hotel this morning?" asked Cinnamon.

"She's been here several times during the past few weeks, taking tours with the owner, Clinton Tate, and meeting with the hotel manager, Glen Durst," replied Gordon. "I don't know what was going on, but if the owner was involved, it must have been something big."

"Do you mean she was planning a big event?"

"No one told me anything about an event, which is unusual because I'm responsible for the food orders and preparations for large events. Maybe it was something else, but it must have been high priority."

"Then I need to find out what it was," she said. "Thanks for your time, Gordon. If you hear anything about the murder, will you call me?"

"Of course."

Cinnamon left the kitchen and ran into Pepper and Curry in the lobby.

"We've been talking to a few of the employees to find out if anyone saw something suspicious involving Maybelle," said Curry.

"Yes," added Pepper, "and we discovered something that might be important. We talked to the housekeeping supervisor. We met her last winter when we donated some clothing from our boutique to a charity event she was chairing. She saw Maybelle arguing with Glen Durst, around nine o'clock this morning outside his office. She couldn't hear what they were saying, but she could tell they were angry."

"That *is* important," agreed Cinnamon. "Did she tell Jason about the argument?"

"Yes, she told him; I'm sure he questioned the manager about it."

"I wonder how we could find out what they were arguing about?" mused Cinnamon.

Pepper and Curry glanced at each other in nervous anticipation. Cinnamon was getting that familiar gleam in her eye. They knew she was concocting another one of her crazy schemes that, more often than not, landed them all in a heap of trouble. Like the time when the twins were eight, and Cinnamon decided they should try parasailing off the roof of the garden shed in the back yard, using their mother's best Damask table cloths. Curry wound up with a broken ankle, and they were all grounded for a month.

The twins could see the wheels turning in Cinnamon's wickedly inventive mind. Never ones to back away from a challenge, in spite of the risks, they waited anxiously to hear the game plan. Their mother's life was at stake here, so they would just have to worry about the consequences later.

And there would be consequences. Too bad their intuition wasn't setting off alarms and flashing red lights, warning them to back off. They had no idea at this point the magnitude of evil that was unleashed on their quiet little community. But they were about to find out—first hand.

Chapter Two

Across town, in a new subdivision of multi-million-dollar mansions, Sage rang the doorbell at the home of Maybelle Jamison. A maid ushered her into a small sitting room where she waited for Cynthia to arrive. Her cell phone rang. It was Cinnamon.

"I didn't have much luck with my search in the hotel kitchen," she said. "Gordon told me Maybelle has been meeting with the hotel owner and manager. He thinks something big was in the works, but doesn't know what it was."

"I'll ask Cynthia," offered Sage. "Surely she knows what her mother was planning, if it was that important."

"Good," replied Cinnamon. "Cynthia is probably the only source we have for checking up on Maybelle's plans. But, Pepper and Curry found out something important. The housekeeping supervisor told them Maybelle had an argument with Glen Durst, the hotel manager, this morning. We need to find out what they were arguing about. He could be a possible murder suspect."

"We'll definitely add him to the list," agreed Sage. "Did the supervisor tell Jason about Maybelle's argument?"

"Yes, I'm sure he's following up on that lead, too."

"I hope so," replied Sage. "I'm at Maybelle's house waiting to talk to Cynthia. Let me see what I can find out here, and then I'll meet you back at the hotel."

"Sure. We'll hang around here and have lunch. Maybe we can pick up some more info. Call me when you leave Maybelle's house."

"Will do," said Sage, hanging up her phone, as Cynthia entered the room.

"Thank you for seeing me, Cynthia," she said, giving her grieving friend a warm hug. "I know how upset you must be over your mother's death."

"We're all still in shock, Sage," said Cynthia, blotting tears from her red, swollen eyes. "Why would someone want to murder my mother? I know she was overbearing and self-centered, but that's no reason to kill her."

"Do you know why she was at the hotel this morning?"

"Yes. She was planning to buy the hotel from Clinton Tate. He put the property on the market a couple of months ago, and Mother became absolutely obsessed with the idea of owning it. She needed a new pet project to occupy her time; and when she found out Clinton wanted to sell the hotel, nothing was going to keep her from getting it. She even had the insane idea that she wanted to run it herself."

"You mean she didn't want to have a manager?"

"Exactly. It was a crazy idea. Mother didn't know the first thing about managing a hotel, not to mention the fact that she would need to give up all her charity projects."

"Did she tell Glen Durst about her plans?"

"Who is Glen Durst?"

"He's the current manager at the hotel. I just found out that Maybelle had an argument with Glen this morning, but we don't know what the argument was about."

"And you think he killed her?"

"Well, most people wouldn't go that far to keep their jobs, but stranger things have happened. You're an attorney—I'm sure you've seen plenty of weirdoes in court."

"You're right about that," Cynthia said. "What are you going to do now?"

"My sisters are waiting for me at the hotel. I'm going to see what I can do to check out Glen Durst."

"Aren't you going to tell the Sheriff?" asked Cynthia

"You mean you haven't told him about your mother's plan to buy the hotel?"

"Not yet. He's supposed to come by later this afternoon."

Sage smiled. "Sure, I'll tell him," she lied. She really did plan to tell him, just not right away; maybe later, after she had a chance to do a little more sleuthing. "I'm going to try my best to find out who killed Maybelle, Cynthia, for her sake as well as my mother's."

"Thank you, Sage. I appreciate anything you can do."

"No thanks necessary," Sage said. "You'd do the same thing for me."

Cynthia smiled bravely, as her puffy eyes began to tear-up again.

"Call me if there's anything I can do to help you get through this nightmare," offered Sage, remembering the fact that she had three sisters and two loving parents to help cushion life's blows; but Cynthia was an only child, whose parents, for the most part, were self-absorbed and totally absent. Even more incentive to catch this killer, she thought, as she returned to her car. She dialed Cinnamon's cell phone. "Stay there. I'm on my way."

Sage made a beeline for the hotel and met her sisters inside the restaurant, where they were chowing down on Friday's lunch special—Seafood Bisque with tiny herb biscuits and a side of fresh fruit salad.

"That looks yummy," remarked Sage.

"It's scrumptious," said Cinnamon, scooping up a steamy spoonful of the fragrant soup. "Gordon really knows his way around seafood, and the spices are perfect."

"Want a bite?" asked Pepper

"No thanks. I'm stuffed," replied Sage. While Cinnamon, Pepper and Curry finished off their lunch, Sage told them about Maybelle's plans to buy the hotel and possibly fire Glen Durst.

"I guess that's what they were arguing about this morning," said Cinnamon. "Do you think he would kill her because of that?"

"I have no idea," admitted Sage. "But right now, he's our only suspect, and I intend to search his office. If he killed Maybelle, he might have hidden the knife there. The deputies have searched everywhere and didn't find it."

"That's what Gordon said, too," added Cinnamon. "Let's check it out."

"How are you going to search his office without him knowing about it?" asked Pepper.

"We'll need a diversion," replied Sage. "You and Curry think up a way to get Glen out of his office for at least thirty minutes. Cinnamon, you can stand guard in the hallway and let me know if anyone is coming, while I search Glen's office."

It never occurred to Sage's three siblings to question her plans. If she decided they needed to search Glen's office, then that's exactly what they would do. As their unofficial leader, they had every confidence that Sage knew what she was doing—most of the time.

Pepper and Curry conferred for a moment over how to accomplish their mission, and then left the restaurant, heading for Glen Durst's office. Sage and Cinnamon kept their fingers crossed that the twins could entice him from his lair. Glen was in his mid-thirties, average height, and somewhat of a geek; but he was a typical male. He wouldn't be able to resist the attention of not one, but two tall, shapely brunettes.

Pepper and Curry turned down careers in fashion modeling, choosing instead to open an upscale clothing boutique in Houston, selling expensive designer clothing, as well as their own original designs. The "Grand Opening" for Panache was held last fall to celebrate their 27th birthdays. They are quite a team, and their sisters didn't doubt for a minute they would launch their own successful line of clothing in the very near future.

Shortly after the twins left the restaurant, Glen strolled through the lobby with Pepper hanging onto one arm and Curry draped over the other. He was all smiles and basking in their glow. As soon as the trio was safely out of sight, Sage and Cinnamon made a dash for Glen's office. Cinnamon took up her station outside the office door, while Sage sneaked inside to begin her search.

She tackled the desk first, opening drawers and rifling through the contents, even checking to make sure nothing was taped to the backs. The only evidence she discovered was not murderous but erotic—a copy of *Penthouse Magazine* in the bottom drawer. "Shame on you, Glen, and on company time, too." Next she moved over to the filing cabinet, flipping through all the folders, but found nothing suspicious; just the usual business correspondence, schedules and memos.

The book cases were last. Sage fanned through each book, hoping to find something inside. Fortunately, Glen wasn't big on reading, so his library was limited. As she opened one of the books on the last shelf, a folded piece of paper fluttered to the floor.

She unfolded the elegant stationery and discovered a Chicago newspaper clipping inside. The headline read "Local Man Embezzles $5,000,000 and Disappears". There beside the headline was a picture of Glen Durst, but the name printed underneath his picture was David Groves. Double shame on you, Glen, she thought. That little geek had managed to pull off a multi-million-dollar heist and get away with it.

Sage scanned the brief, hand-written letter. It was from Maybelle. "I don't want any scandal attached to this hotel," the letter read. "Withdraw your purchase offer and move on quietly, so I won't be forced to reveal your true identity."

"Whew," whistled Sage. "Now there's a motive for murder. They both wanted to buy this hotel, and Maybelle was using blackmail to gain the upper hand." Sage had no idea why Maybelle would commit a Federal crime to get what she wanted, but Cynthia was right about her mother being obsessed with the idea of owning this hotel.

Unfortunately, Maybelle miscalculated the consequences of her actions, and look what that mistake had cost her. But if Glen killed Maybelle, where did he hide the murder weapon? Sage had turned that office inside out and not found it. Frustrated, she plopped down in the desk chair, staring blankly at the serene oil painting hanging on the wall in front of her.

"Oh," she said, jumping up from the chair. "Of course, why didn't I think of it before?"

*   *   *   *   *   *   *   *   *   *

Sheriff Jason Winters and Deputy Sam Davis climbed the main staircase in the hotel lobby in search of Glen Durst. After conducting a lengthy background check on the otherwise mild-mannered hotel manager, the Sheriff had turned up some rather unsavory news. Apparently Mr. Durst had sticky fingers when it came to other people's money.

The front desk clerk had directed the two lawmen to the second floor. "He's in the Magnolia Ballroom," she said, "assisting two clients plan for an event."

As they reached the top of the stairs, they spotted the hotel manager chatting amiably with Pepper and Curry McCormick. He was giggling like a chubby little kid on a roller coaster, as the spice twins flirted with him shamelessly.

"I smell a rat!" said Jason. "If Pepper and Curry are here, then Sage and Cinnamon can't be far behind."

"Who?" asked the confused deputy.

"I think what we've got here is a diversionary tactic. That means Sage must be stalking Glen Durst, and I've got a good idea where to find her."

Jason dashed down the stairs, taking them two at a time, with the puzzled deputy struggling to keep up. He knew he'd find that nosey barrister snooping around in Glen's office.

Meanwhile, Sage, who was completely unaware of the whirlwind bearing down upon her, ran around the desk and lifted the large oil painting off the wall. She turned it over, and there, taped to the back of the canvas, was a plastic bag holding a large steak knife.

She shuddered at the traces of blood still visible on the blade, thinking how shocked poor Maybelle must have felt when her attacker struck—first pain, then outrage and finally the fear of losing her life as she struggled to reach the staircase.

Outside the office door, she heard Cinnamon's voice, "Jason. What are you doing here?"

Before Sage could react, Jason burst into the office, glaring at the back of the painting she still held in both hands.

"Your finger prints had better not be on that bag," he warned.

"Do I look that stupid?" she countered. "I should think you'd be grateful that I discovered the murder weapon and the motive," she added, nodding at the letter on the desk.

"I was already on my way to arrest David Groves," he replied. "I can't just break into people's offices—I have to go through the proper legal channels and actually take the time to get warrants."

"I didn't break in," argued Sage. "The door was open."

"And you think that gives you the right—legal or otherwise—to go poking around in someone's private space?"

"When my mother's life is at stake, yes, I do!"

David Groves, a.k.a. Glen Durst, stepped into the office, "What are you doing in here? Get out of my office!"

"It's too late for that," said Jason, holding up a warrant. "David Groves, I'm arresting you for embezzlement. Read him his rights, Sam; then take him down to the station."

Deputy Davis hauled off the confounded Glen Durst, as Cinnamon, Pepper and Curry gathered outside the office door.

"Embezzlement?" asked the equally confounded Sage. "What about murder?"

"Unfortunately, you didn't do your homework, Counselor. Glen Durst has an airtight alibi for Maybelle Jamison's murder. He was in a meeting with a room full of people when she was stabbed," explained Jason.

"But what about the blackmail letter from Maybelle?" argued Sage, holding up the letter for Jason to scan.

"He might have had motive," agreed Jason, "but he didn't have opportunity."

"Maybe he hired someone to do it," offered Sage, in a desperate attempt to make her theory fit.

"I intend to explore that possibility, but, in the mean time, I expect you to keep your nose out of my investigation."

Cinnamon, Pepper and Curry, standing outside the office door, stepped back, anticipating the inevitable fireworks from yet another Sage and Jason confrontation.

Sage's bright green eyes glittered with anger. Her three sisters gasped and backed up again. Pulling herself up to her full five feet, four inches—in heels—she glared up at Jason—a good ten inches taller.

"Not a chance in hell!" she growled. "Not as long as my mother is a murder suspect!"

"Dammit, Sage," said the exasperated Sheriff. "You know I don't believe your mother killed anybody, but this is a murder investigation, and I have to follow all the leads—no matter where that takes me."

"Then you can expect me to be following leads, too," countered Sage. "I know you're a good investigator, Jason, but this is my mother we're talking about. I will not stop until this case is solved."

Jason sighed. He might as well be arguing with a brick wall. "You can't do much investigating from behind bars, and that's exactly where you're going to wind up if you keep breaking into offices and tampering with evidence."

"Humph," mumbled Sage, putting her hands on her hips in defiance. But her belligerent stance was just a bluff. She knew he could toss her skinny ass in jail if she didn't play her cards right.

"Can I count on you not to break any more laws?" he asked.

Sage paused briefly, her knees feeling limp under the gaze of his smoky brown eyes. She wasn't about to make any promises at this stage of the game, so she gave a quick nod instead. The trick here was not to get caught. She'd just have to be more careful in the future.

"I know asking you to be patient is like asking you not to breathe," added Jason. "Just give me a chance, and I promise I'll find this killer."

Sage relaxed a bit. She knew Jason was doing his best, but it couldn't hurt to have a backup investigation; and there was no way in hell she could sit around and wait. Once again, she nodded, without making a verbal commitment.

"Truce?" asked Jason, with a guarded smile.

"Truce," replied Sage, feeling like a tap dancer on a tight rope.

Cinnamon, Pepper and Curry breathed a sigh of relief—another battle with no bloodshed—now that was progress.

Chapter Three

Jason packed up the blackmail letter and murder weapon that Sage uncovered during her quasi-legal search of Glen Durst's office, and left the scene. Sage and her sisters, disheartened to learn that their prime suspect in Maybelle's murder had an airtight alibi, returned to the hotel lobby to rethink their strategy.

"Now what?" asked Cinnamon. "If Glen Durst isn't the killer, we're back to square one."

"Not necessarily," replied Sage. "We don't know for sure he's not the killer. He could easily have hired someone to murder Maybelle."

"So how are we supposed to check out that possibility?" asked Pepper. "Hired assassins aren't exactly listed in the Yellow Pages."

"I guess we'll have to leave that part of the investigation up to Jason," admitted Sage. "The deputies have contacts and informants who can check that out. What we can do though, is find out more about Maybelle—talk to her friends, neighbors, acquaintances and family to see if she had any other enemies. If she resorted to blackmail to get what she wanted from Glen, she's probably pissed off a few more people in the past."

"That could take forever," complained Cinnamon. "Maybelle Jamison practically ran this town."

"Mother might be able to help," offered Curry. "She's lived here as long as Maybelle."

"That's true," agreed Sage. "Let's go back to the hospital."

* * * * * * * * * *

Once again, the four sisters converged on the nursing station in the ER, where Nurse Crane was packing up to leave for the day.

"Oh, Lord," she said, when she realized the spice group had returned.

"What happened to our mother?" asked Sage. "The exam room is empty."

"They're moving her to Three-South," replied the nurse, nervously checking her watch. Just six more minutes and her shift was over. She had actually managed to make it through the rest of the day without any more weirdoes showing up—until now, at least. Just six more Friday minutes, and she could go home and put up her tired, sore feet and forget about this loony bin for the entire weekend.

"So which room is she in on Three-South?" asked Sage.

"She's not in any room yet," said Nurse Crane. "She... Did you say empty?" she frowned, looking from the spice sisters to the hallway and back. "Maybe you checked the wrong exam room," she smiled, mentally ticking off the seconds.

"We can read," argued Cinnamon, her spiky reddish hair vibrating with irritation. "Room number four is empty."

Nurse Crane bounded out from behind the desk and waddled as fast as her short legs could carry her down the hallway, with the spice group tight on her heels. She pushed open the door to exam room four and pulled up short at the sight of the empty bed. The four sisters piled into her before they could stop.

"You don't know where she is?" asked Sage, grabbing onto the nurse to keep her from falling after their abrupt collision.

"Stand back," demanded Nurse Crane, fighting her way back through the tiny, crowded space. She hit the hallway at a gallop this time, with the sisters hanging back at a safer distance.

She grabbed the phone on the desk and punched in a few numbers. "Sandra," she said, gasping for air. "Did you send someone to pick up the patient in exam room four, Ginger McCormick?" The nurse winced at the stitch in her side—she wasn't accustomed to doing the fifty-yard dash during her shift. Damn these people! They weren't supposed to move her patients without telling her. As if this job wasn't stressful enough, now she had to play detective and track down the whereabouts of her patients.

The four sisters stood in wide-eyed silence while Nurse Crane waited for a response.

"No," replied Sandra, the equally frustrated nurse on Three-South. "Just keep your panties on. We don't have a room ready yet. We're packed to the gills up here and can't get these damned doctors off the golf course long enough to release their patients. Are you backing up down there in ER?"

Nurse Crane paused with a heavy sigh. "No. We're good. I'll get back to you later."

She hung up the phone and drummed her short, chubby fingers on the desk. Now what? Four anxious family members on the verge of hysteria were standing right in front of her, expecting an answer—now. "I don't know" was not an option at this point.

"If you ladies will just have a seat in the waiting area," she said as calmly as she could, "I'll make a few calls and we'll get this cleared up."

* * * * * * * * * *

The wary sisters made their way over to the sparsely populated waiting area, claiming a row of alternating turquoise and burnt orange vinyl upholstered chairs, while they awaited the verdict. They had no choice really—what else could they do?

"I don't like this one bit," complained Pepper, trying to keep her voice low, in spite of her mounting concern.

"Somebody screwed up big time," snarled Cinnamon, sliding down in her seat and propping both feet on the magazine-littered coffee table. "And now they're trying to cover their butts."

"Let's call Dad," said Sage. "Maybe he knows something."

* * * * * * * * * *

An exasperated Nurse Crane called the Chief Administrator to put out an alert for a missing patient. Did she leave the hospital against medical advice? She was supposed to stay overnight for observation, but not everyone agreed to follow doctors' orders.

Somehow the nurse didn't think this was the case for Ginger McCormick. A shiver ran down her spine. That nagging premonition was back, but this time it wasn't for herself. She had a bad feeling about Ginger McCormick's disappearance. This situation was going to get worse before it got better—if it got better.

* * * * * * * * * *

"Dad?" said Sage, when Mace answered the phone. "Did you check Mother out of the hospital? Is she home with you?"

"What are you talking about?" he asked. "The hospital staff said they were going to move her up to Three-South. I came back to work for a while and planned to return to the hospital tonight to visit her. Did you check with the nurse?"

"Yeah," replied Sage, slowly, not wanting to alarm her father. "The hospital is checking into it now to see if they can locate her."

"What do you mean—locate her?" he cried. "The hospital has lost your mother? Oh my God!"

"Calm down, Dad. I didn't say they lost her. I said they're checking into..." Click. The phone call was terminated abruptly by an overwrought Mace.

"Well, damn!" said Sage.

"What did he say?" asked Cinnamon.

"Did he check Mother out of the hospital?" asked Pepper.

"No," replied Sage. "He didn't check her out and now he's gone ballistic over the news that she's missing. It will be a miracle if he doesn't stroke out before he gets here. At least, I assume he's coming here—he didn't really say."

"What a mess!" exclaimed Curry, on the verge of tears. "What could have happened to Mother?"

For the first time in her life, Sage's "damn the torpedoes, full speed ahead" attitude had deserted her. She had no response to that question.

"Ms. McCormick," said a short, slightly plump, balding man.

"Yes," replied all four sisters in unison.

"Oh," he raised his dark, bushy eyebrows in surprise as he surveyed the motley group of young women. "I'm Norman Spears, the hospital's Chief Administrator. We seem to have a slight miscommunication involving Ginger McCormick, who is your mother, I understand?"

"Miscommunication?" squeaked Cinnamon, as mounting anger turned her otherwise creamy-white complexion three shades of red. "Is that the official term for losing one of your patients?"

Sage rested her hand gently on Cinnamon's arm, hoping to thwart a nasty confrontation—at least until they determined the appropriate target for their combined wrath. "Yes, Ginger McCormick is our mother," she replied, willing herself to remain calm. "We just spoke to our father, who told us he did not check her out of this hospital; so she must be here somewhere."

"Right," confirmed Norman, nervously pulling a white handkerchief from the pocket of his dark pin-striped suit and blotting a trickle of perspiration running down the side of his bald head. "Our records also indicate that she has not checked out."

"So, what's next?" asked Sage, trying not to jump to any conclusions. "Could she have been moved to a different floor of the hospital by mistake?"

"We've already checked all the nursing stations," he replied, tugging uncomfortably at the heavily starched collar of his white business shirt. "Unfortunately, none of them received a patient from the ER this afternoon."

All four sisters stared at him in silence, trying to understand the implications of this news. They looked at each other, then back at Norman, waiting for another explanation—anything but "she's gone and we don't know where she is."

Norman understood the pleading stares. "Is there any chance that she might have left the hospital on her own?" he asked futilely.

"Oh, my God!" cried Curry. "She's been kidnapped!"

At that moment, all hell broke loose. Pepper and Curry began to sob uncontrollably. Cinnamon launched into a tirade, screaming at Norman Spears about hospital negligence and security incompetence. Sage whipped out her cell phone and called 911 to report a kidnapping.

Nurse Crane, deciding there was nothing more she could do to stop this avalanche, sneaked out the back entrance, trying desperately to save her own sanity.

* * * * * * * * * *

Jason and Mace arrived at the entrance to the ER at the same time.

"Ginger's been kidnapped?" asked Jason.

"She has?" replied Mace, in horror.

The two men stared at each other in a moment of confusion, as three more deputies arrived on the scene. They all tumbled through the ER doors into total chaos.

The chief of hospital security, Dan Bartels, who had arrived just moments before, was backed into a corner by four hysterical daughters and one frantic administrator—all demanding the return of the missing Ginger. Upon Jason's arrival, the entire group transferred their angst onto the beleaguered Sheriff; as Mace tried desperately to get an update on Ginger's status.

"Stop!" yelled Jason. "I can't understand a thing any of you is saying. Norman, tell me what's going on here."

"Ginger McCormick is missing," replied the frazzled administrator. "She didn't check out of the hospital, she wasn't moved to another floor, and no one saw her leave."

"Oh, no," cried Mace, sinking down onto one of the waiting room chairs. His daughters rushed over to comfort him. Sage held his hand, trying to reassure him that everything would be okay, while Cinnamon fanned his pale face with a dog-eared copy of *Woman's Day Magazine*, fearing he would pass out from shock.

"What have you got so far?" Jason asked Dan.

"Nothing—I just got here, but I plan to check the videotapes in the security cameras."

"Let's do it," ordered Jason. "The rest of you wait here. We'll be back as soon as we can."

Once again, Sage locked eyes with Jason. Only this time, her eyes were pleading for help. He understood, and gave her a slight nod before racing up the stairs to the security office.

* * * * * * * * * *

Dan pulled the videotape for the ER exam room hallway and put it into the tape player. He pushed the fast forward button to advance the tape to the afternoon footage. The two officers watched as the ER staff went about their usual routine, taking patients in and out of the various exam rooms; but their attention was focused on exam room number four.

Around three o'clock, Mace left the room. At 3:15, a man wearing a hospital scrub suit wheeled an empty laundry cart slowly down the hallway. A scrub cap covered his hair, and he kept his head lowered to avoid a direct view from the security camera.

Jason and Dan moved to the edge of their seats, intently watching his every move. After pausing in front of room number four, he glanced in each direction down the hallway and pushed the cart into the room.

Each officer held his breath as they waited for the man to emerge. Finally, the door opened. The suspect checked to make sure the hallway was empty, and then pulled the laundry cart out of the room. There was a large, white bag inside, and it was much too big to be a laundry bag. Jason and Dan stared at each other in stunned silence, and then watched as the man wheeled the cart slowly down the hallway toward the exit.

All Jason could think about at that moment was, "How am I going to tell Sage?"

They returned to the ER to deliver the bad news about Ginger's kidnapping, feeling certain that she was in the laundry cart the suspect wheeled out the back exit to the hospital delivery parking lot. The parking lot camera recorded him loading the cart into the back of a black van, but the license tags were covered to prevent identification. They weren't dealing with amateurs. These kidnappers had their act together.

* * * * * * * * * *

"We believe she was taken out of the hospital in a laundry cart and loaded into a black van," Jason told the incredulous family members, who stared at him in helpless shock.

"Why would someone kidnap Mother?" asked Cinnamon.

"It couldn't be for money," added Mace.

"It has to be Maybelle's killer," surmised Sage, her criminal lawyer mind rapidly clicking the tumblers into place. "He thinks Mother saw or heard something at the murder scene."

Jason nodded sadly to confirm his agreement with her theory.

"The killer has Mother?" cried Curry, sobbing once again. "Is he going to kill her, too?"

Mace dropped his face into his hands, stricken with grief and fear.

"I've already issued an APB on the van," said Jason, trying his best to offer hope in what appeared to be a hopeless situation. "There's nothing more you can do here, Mace. I think it's best for you to go home now, in case the kidnapper calls. I have a deputy assigned to stay with you. We've called in extra police officers from the surrounding areas to help with the search. We'll find her," he added, trying to sound more confident than he felt.

Mace nodded sadly and left the hospital, escorted by one of the deputies. He had never felt so helpless in his entire life. Just when he managed to recover from this morning's heart-stopping scare, he was hit with another life-threatening blow. How could this be happening? He had to do something to save Ginger. But what could he do? And then he smiled, remembering his four beautiful, intelligent and resourceful daughters. "We're on our way, Honey," he whispered. He knew in his heart that, with his daughters' help, he would find Ginger and bring her home safely.

Jason switched into high-gear, barking orders to his deputies, as they tripped over each other in their haste to carry out their life-saving missions. "Sage, get me a recent photo of your mother. We'll hand out flyers and give notices to all the local T.V. and radio stations."

Sage jumped up, glad to have this assignment to boost her morale. She promised to e-mail a photo to the Sheriff's office within the hour and gathered her sisters around her to plan their search strategy. She was a fighter—she wasn't about to give up yet.

Jason saw the hope in her eyes and knew she was back on board. That's what he loved about her—that feisty spirit. Hell, at this point, he didn't care if she broke into offices and tampered with evidence. He could use all the help he could get.

Chapter Four

Ginger's eyes fluttered open. She tried to focus on a large, dark shape beside her bed in the dimly lit room, but her head ached and she felt groggy. Why was it so dark in the exam room? Why was it so quiet? She could no longer hear the constant, familiar noise of the bustling emergency room—the murmuring sounds of the doctor/nurse conferences, the non-stop buzzing of the nurse call buttons, the constant ping of the elevator bell, followed by the sound of sliding doors, and the occasional cry of a patient in pain.

She continued to stare at the object beside her bed. For some reason, the room seemed larger, but it was so dark. Where was Mace? He said he would come back to visit her after work. As the object beside her bed slowly began to take shape, she realized it was an ornately carved chest of drawers. How odd, she thought. Maybe she was dreaming.

"Oh!" she cried, suddenly sitting upright on her bed. "Ow!" she screeched, as her cracked ribs dug into her bruised side. Gently, she lay back down on the bed, taking short breaths until the sharp pain subsided. Fear crept into the recesses of her foggy memory. Frightening images flashed through her brain: a man standing over her hospital bed, the smell of a strong chemical as he covered her nose and mouth with a thick cloth, the fear she felt as she fought desperately to breathe, then total darkness as her world went black for the second time in one day.

Finally, she realized she was no longer in the hospital exam room. She had a vague recollection of waking up inside a moving vehicle, but, at the time, she was completely covered by white fabric. All she could see was light filtering through the cloth. Her hands and feet were bound and a gag was stuffed into her mouth. Then, she lost consciousness again.

Ginger didn't remember being moved into this room, but her hands and feet were no longer bound and the gag was gone. She reached out to turn on the bedside lamp. A soft warm glow illuminated the elegantly furnished room. It looked like a picture from a decorating magazine. It was typical of Ginger's luck to be snatched by a wealthy kidnapper and held in a luxurious...What was this place? Was she in someone's house? She listened intently for any sound, and heard the faint cries of seagulls overhead.

She glanced over at the narrow window, covered with heavy draperies. An orange glow peeked through the crack where the curtains were drawn closed. Ginger rose from the queen-size bed, but more gently this time to avoid the sharp, stabbing pain from her ribs. Barefoot, she walked across the plush carpet and pulled back the curtain.

The setting sun glistened off the water of Pelican Bay far below. She looked down at the parking lot in front of the building—it was The Grand Hotel. But she had never seen this room before. She and Mace had stayed at the hotel several times to celebrate their anniversary. As a wedding consultant, she had toured all twelve of the luxurious guest rooms on the third floor, but this room was higher up. She knew there was a private residence on the fourth floor, tucked under the steep roofline of the building. This room must be part of the residence area.

Ginger turned and crossed the room to the door. It was locked from the outside. Of course—what did she expect? It was an elegant and comfortable space, but she was still a prisoner. Why would someone want to kidnap her? She and Mace weren't wealthy. They couldn't afford to pay a huge ransom. What could this person hope to gain from kidnapping her?

Her thoughts turned to Mace and her four daughters. They must be sick with worry. Would she ever see them again, she wondered, as tears welled up in her eyes?

"No!" she cried, anger replacing her fear. "I'm not giving in to helplessness. I will find a way out of here." Ginger was a feisty little fireball, too, just like her daughter, Sage. She began to feel like herself again—energetic, resourceful, and confident. Her determination to be reunited with her family gave her strength.

The wheels began to turn in her creative mind, as she sat in the middle of her silk-draped bed and plotted her escape, but from whom? She had no idea who she was up against. She scanned the room, looking for clues that would give her some inkling of her kidnapper's intentions, when her gaze fell on the fluffy white bath robe draped over the end of the bed. It dawned on her that she was still wearing a hospital gown—the one with the air conditioned vent down the back. Well, that was a clue. Her kidnapper was concerned about her modesty. How odd.

* * * * * * * * * *

The four McCormick sisters left the ER, headed for their parents' house to set up their investigation headquarters. Without Ginger's help, the fact-gathering mission would be considerably more difficult, but a sense of urgency forced them to forge ahead.

Sitting in the well-worn, but comfortable, over-stuffed chairs in the McCormick's cozy family room, the sisters made their plans. Mace, excited that the investigation process was in full swing, dashed into the kitchen to whip up a batch of his famous spicy-hot chili and a pan of jalapeño cornbread to serve his daughters for dinner. He busied himself chopping and cooking while his daughters began to strategize.

"We need to make a list of possible suspects," said Sage. "Who would have a reason to murder Maybelle?"

"I guess we can rule out Glen Durst," suggested Cinnamon. "He could have hired someone to kill her, but I doubt that he would kidnap Mother—especially since he's in jail now."

"Unfortunately, that's true. It looks like he's off the hook as far as Maybelle's murder is concerned," replied Sage, reluctantly.

"What about her husband, Henry Jamison?" asked Curry. "He's a big-time real estate developer and a U.S. Representative. Maybe he had a reason to get rid of her—especially in light of his most recent political scandal involving an affair with another woman in Washington, D.C. I know his assistant, Sharon Daniels. She might be able to help."

"The husband is always a possibility," agreed Sage. "You take care of investigating him. Who else?"

"Why don't I question the chairwomen for some of the charity committees Maybelle was on," offered Cinnamon. "My restaurant has catered several of their events. I'm sure they would want to help—for Maybelle's sake, as well as Mother's."

"That's a good idea," replied Sage. "I'm sure they would know all the latest gossip. What about you, Pepper? Do you have any ideas to add?"

"I think I should go back to the hotel and continue talking to the employees there," replied Pepper. "Maybe someone saw or heard something unusual that they didn't report before. Now that there's a kidnapping associated with the murder, maybe it will jog a memory."

"Good plan," agreed Sage. "See what you can turn up at the hotel." After pausing for a moment, she added, "Perhaps I can check into Clinton Tate's background, along with his network of 'good old boy' business development partners. Since he owned the hotel and was planning to sell it to Maybelle, there might be a connection. Maybe I can unearth a few skeletons."

Curry wiped a tear from the corner of her eye. "Do you think Mother is still alive?"

"I know she is!" said Sage. "That kidnapper met his match when he snatched Ginger McCormick. He got a lot more than he bargained for."

Cinnamon, Pepper and Curry all smiled and nodded. They knew Sage was right.

"Damn straight," confirmed Mace, standing at the dining room table, holding a huge pot of steaming chili. "Come and get it." The girls crowded around the table, as their father ladled the stew into bowls.

"This smells wonderful," said Cinnamon, inhaling the spicy aroma.

"You've outdone yourself, Dad," added Sage, stuffing a large piece of warm cornbread into her mouth. "Yum!"

By the time the sisters ate dinner and finished their detective plans, it was late. They all bunked down in the guest rooms at their childhood home. Going back to Houston that night was not an option. Their father needed their support, and they wanted to be close by in case the deputies found their mother.

Planning to start their search bright and early the next morning, the family members each sent up a silent prayer that they would find Ginger, alive and well; and then fell into a restless but desperately needed sleep.

* * * * * * * * * *

On the fourth floor of The Grand Hotel, Ginger sat in the middle of her luxurious bed, wondering if she would ever see her family again, when she heard a soft knock on the door to her room. A polite kidnapper? Puzzled and frightened, she grabbed the robe off the end of the bed and slipped it on.

"Yes?" she replied, nervously.

The door opened and an attractive young man entered the room. He wore neatly pressed dark slacks and a freshly laundered long-sleeve white shirt, with the sleeves rolled up to his elbows. He carried a dinner tray emitting an aroma so tantalizing that Ginger's mouth began to water.

"We thought you might be hungry," he said.

Ginger stood silently by the edge of the bed, her eyes wide with fear and her heart pounding like a hammer.

"There's no reason for you to be afraid," assured the man. "Please come and sit down, and I'll try to explain the situation." He motioned toward the desk where he placed the tray.

Ginger didn't move. Situation? He thinks kidnapping is a situation? Her face flushed with anger and her fear vanished as she opened her mouth to protest—well, actually throw a hissy fit!

But the polite young man held up his hand, "Please, just let me explain. You really should try to remain calm because of your injuries. I'm with the F.B.I. We've taken over the fourth floor of The Grand Hotel for an undercover surveillance operation, and we're holding you here for your own protection."

Ginger's mouth fell open in disbelief. "Protection?" she finally managed to squeak.

"Yes," he replied, taking a step toward Ginger.

She quickly backed away from him, slamming into the dresser and winced at the pain in her ribs. "Damn," she cried, grabbing her side, now angrier than ever. "Show me your I.D."

"I'm Special Agent Peter Dalton," he replied, pulling his I.D. folder from his pants pocket and flipping it open for her to see.

"Please, Ginger, come and have a seat at the desk before you hurt yourself."

She frowned as she studied the picture on the I.D. then nodded. "F.B.I.?"

Peter sighed and motioned for her to be seated.

She sat down in the desk chair as Peter lifted the silver dome off a steaming plate of pasta, sprinkled with chunks of grilled chicken and steamed veggies, tossed with a creamy white sauce. Ginger nearly swooned from the aroma. She was starving.

Peter smiled and sat down in an upholstered chair beside the desk.

"Oh," moaned Ginger, scooping up a mouthful of the delectable concoction. "This is heavenly. I don't recall this dish being on the menu here at the hotel."

"It isn't," replied Peter. "We can't have food brought up from the hotel kitchen. It would be too risky to have that much traffic through here. Since one of the hotel employees is our suspect, the hotel owner was told that his guest is a wealthy celebrity who needs the entire floor for her entourage and doesn't require any services from the hotel staff."

"Then where did you get this food?" asked Ginger, looking at the elegant china and silver cover.

"I made it," replied Peter. "I enjoy cooking when I have the time, and this suite has a fully equipped kitchen."

"I think you missed your calling," said Ginger. "You should be a chef like my daughter."

"It's on my agenda for retirement," he admitted, "which, in this business, comes pretty early."

Temporarily distracted by her moment of instant food gratification, Ginger soon snapped back to the crisis at hand.

"What do you mean my protection?" she asked.

"Our field office in Houston is investigating a person in the area who is suspected of selling arms to a terrorist group."

"Terrorists? Here in Clearwater?" asked Ginger, her fork poised in mid-air.

"The dealer and his associates are in Clearwater," replied Peter. "We've been following leads for months and Maybelle Jamison's death was the final piece of the puzzle we needed."

"Maybelle was an arms dealer?"

"No," chuckled Peter. "We have reason to believe the dealer is an employee at this hotel. Unfortunately, Maybelle stumbled across some information that could expose him. That's why she was murdered."

Ginger closed her eyes, thinking about poor Maybelle; then turned a questioning gaze on Peter, "With a steak knife?"

Peter's intelligent blue eyes reflected a growing respect for this feisty, petite woman and her attention for details.

"That was a cover," he explained. "This group is highly sophisticated and well trained. They couldn't allow Maybelle's death to look like an assassination, but that's exactly what it was."

"How do you know all this?"

"Because we have a mole planted in their group."

"Well, if you know who they are, why don't you arrest them?"

"We need to find the leader of the group."

"Your mole doesn't know who he is?"

"He hasn't been able to penetrate the group at that level yet."

"So what did Maybelle learn that caused her...?" Ginger couldn't even say the words. All this cloak and dagger stuff was mind-boggling. But the fact that it was going on right here in Clearwater was just too much to fathom.

"Apparently, she found documentation about the arms dealer's identity. Unfortunately, instead of going to the police, she confronted the dealer, and either he or someone in his group killed her. It looks like they tried to frame the hotel manager for the murder by planting the murder weapon in his office."

"Poor Glen. I hope he wasn't falsely accused of murder."

"Actually, Glen Durst is in jail. His real name is David Groves, and he was arrested this afternoon for embezzling millions of dollars from a Chicago business a few years ago."

"Oh, my. This has been one crazy day—murder, kidnapping, embezzlement. But what does all this have to do with me? Why do you think I need protection?"

"The dealer and his associates are afraid that Maybelle passed along some information before she died. They have to make sure any possible leaks are plugged—permanently."

Ginger gasped. "Maybelle didn't say anything to me before she died. She came rolling down those stairs like a bowling ball and picked me off like a spare pin. Do they think we had time for a friendly chat while we were bumping our way down those rock-hard steps?"

Peter grimaced in sympathy, thinking about Ginger's unfortunate timing. "Are you sure you didn't hear something? Maybe after you landed at the bottom of the stairs—before you blacked out. Think carefully. It could be the clue we need to nab this arms dealer."

Ginger closed her eyes and tried to visualize her fall: her complete surprise at being knocked off her feet, the feeling of total helplessness as she tried desperately to grab onto something to stop the plunge, and the pain of each crushing blow as gravity dragged her body down the jagged plane. But the shock that jarred her brain when her head smacked the granite floor was the worst. Then, mercifully, the pain stopped when she lost consciousness.

She did remember hearing sounds, though. There were people in the lobby at the time. Screams; she heard people screaming, perhaps when they realized what was happening. Or maybe those were her own screams. And... she heard... Yes, she did hear someone say, "Applewhite."

Ginger frowned, deep in thought. "Applewhite," she repeated. "I heard someone say, 'Applewhite.' But I don't remember who said it. Maybe I just dreamed it."

Peter's face went blank, and then turned pale when he heard the name.

"Does that mean anything to you?" asked Ginger, somewhat concerned by his reaction.

"I'll be right back," he said, jumping out of his chair and racing toward the door.

"Wait!" cried Ginger. "You've got to let me out of here. I've already told you everything I know. Please let me go home. My family must be sick with worry."

"They would feel even worse if you were dead," he replied. "You can't leave yet. You have no idea how dangerous these people are."

Ginger began to cry. "Then at least let my family know I'm alive," she pleaded.

"I'm sorry, Ginger. That would compromise our investigation. We can't let anyone know about our surveillance. Please be patient. I will notify your family as soon as I can."

Peter turned to leave, but paused. "We have a nurse coming by later to check on you. Try to get some rest." And then he was gone, with the door locked securely behind him.

Ginger collapsed onto the bed, feeling exhausted and angry. How could this be happening to her? What had she done to deserve this nightmare? There she was just minding her own business, taking care of her bride's wedding plans, when life came along and dumped a load of crap right on top of her.

She had been body slammed, kidnapped and locked in a five-star prison to avoid terrorist assassins. That kind of stuff just doesn't happen in real life! Not her life, at least. She squirmed around on the bed, trying to get comfortable; punching the pricey down pillows and tugging at the 800-thread-count Egyptian cotton sheets until she finally lost the battle with exhaustion.

* * * * * * * * * *

Ginger awoke to the sound of a soft knock at the door. "Yes?" she answered groggily.

A pretty young woman opened the door and peeked inside. "Ginger? I'm Sally Woods, the nurse Peter sent to check on you."

"Oh," said Ginger sitting up in the bed. "Please come in."

"How are you feeling?" asked the nurse, cheerfully. "Have you had any headaches or blurred vision this evening?"

"No," replied Ginger, "just an occasional sharp pain in my chest if I try to move too suddenly."

"That's to be expected," said the nurse. "It will get better soon."

Nurse Woods took Ginger's blood pressure, pulse and temperature. "Everything looks fine. I brought you a clean gown and some slippers. Would you like me to help you take a bath?"

"That would be wonderful," said Ginger. "But what about the tape on my ribs."

"I'll take it off temporarily and replace it when you're finished bathing. Just try to keep the cast on your arm out of the water."

The nurse filled the huge soaking tub with warm water and added the expensive bubble bath the hotel supplied for its guests, while Ginger took off her gown and slipped into the heavenly warm, scented bath.

She leaned back in the tub and closed her eyes, trying as best as she could to forget about the turmoil surrounding her. But a shadow fell across her face, and she felt pressure on both shoulders. She opened her eyes to see Nurse Woods standing over her, smiling as she forced Ginger's head down under the swirling bubbles.

She thrashed about wildly trying to escape the woman's grasp. How could this be happening? She was supposed to be safe in the protective custody of the F.B.I. for God's sake! But instead, she was fighting for her life with the "nurse from hell"! In a last ditch effort, she pushed her feet against the front of the tub, using every ounce of energy she could muster, forcing her head out of the water just long enough to scream.

Where was Peter? Was he close enough to hear her? The nurse pushed her down into the water again, but Ginger had no strength left, and the searing pain in her chest was more than she could bear.

Chapter Five

Ginger couldn't hold her breath any longer; her lungs felt like they would burst. Nurse Woods was too strong, and her injuries had already drained the last of her reserves. This is it, she thought, as she began to lose consciousness—I'm going to die.

Suddenly, the hands holding her under water let go, and she sat up gasping for air. Peter had thrown Nurse Woods halfway across the bathroom floor, slamming her into the vanity. He drew his gun and pointed it at the attacker, as two other agents rushed into the bathroom.

Agents Ted Johnson and Harriet Blair hauled the crumpled nurse out of the room. Peter plopped down on the vanity bench with his head down, trying to compose himself. He hated it when he screwed up. This poor woman's life was in his hands, and he had let her down.

"I'm so sorry, Ginger," he panted, still breathing hard from the scuffle. "We just discovered the real nurse tied up in a closet downstairs."

Ginger couldn't even reply. She was shaken to the core by her life-threatening ordeal, trembling with fear, and trying to cough up the water in her lungs, which made her chest pain more severe. Her perfectly coiffed auburn hair now hung in a crown of dripping ringlets. How could her life get any worse? Oh, yeah, she was sitting in a bathtub, naked in front of a total stranger. The only good part was that she had actually managed to keep the cast on her arm dry during the entire near-death incident. Thank God for small favors.

"I'll send in Agent Blair to help you," offered Peter, realizing her naked dilemma.

Ginger leaned back in the tub, completely exhausted, while Harriet perched on the same bench that Peter had recently vacated.

"Do I have to move now?" asked the comatose Ginger.

"Not until you're ready," replied Harriet.

Ginger frowned, recalling the terrifying scene. "Having to fight for your life in a bubble bath kind of spoils the mood doesn't it?"

"I can see where it might throw a kink in the relaxation part," smiled Harriet, sympathetically.

After Ginger was dried off, robed and planted back in bed, Peter came in to see her.

"If you don't mind," quipped Ginger, "I think I'll just go home and take my chances there."

"This incident should prove just how desperately these people want you dead," countered Peter. "We're doing the best we can to protect you, Ginger, but sometimes our best isn't enough."

Ginger began to cry. "I just want to go home. I want to see my family again."

"You will," promised Peter. "Soon."

Peter called in a doctor to check Ginger over and re-tape her fractured ribs. The doctor gave her a light sedative to help her sleep and tucked her in for the night.

I hope the terrorists have decided to call it a night, too, she thought, as she drifted off to sleep. But I'm getting the hell out of this place.

* * * * * * * * * *

The McCormick sisters rose early the next morning, anxious to start the search for their missing mother. The long, narrow driveway beside the family home looked like a parking lot. All four young women lived in nearby Houston and drove into Clearwater yesterday when they heard about their mother's accident. Each sibling had her own mission in the investigation today. Their plan was to "divide and conquer".

Sage, wearing her usual lawyer costume—a dark business suit, pantyhose and low heels—tossed a leather brief case into her new silver Mercedes and backed down the driveway first. She planned to talk to a former high school buddy, Todd Bailey, who worked at the Clearwater Business Development Center, about Clinton Tate and his partners. Perhaps Maybelle Jamison had turned up some shady deals during her business transaction with Mr. Tate, and he wanted to make sure they weren't exposed.

"Thanks for seeing me on such short notice," said Sage, giving her friend a quick hug.

"I'm glad to help," replied Todd. "I was shocked to hear about Maybelle's murder and then your mother's disappearance. I'm really sorry. What can I do to help?"

"We're doing background checks on anyone who might be considered a murder suspect," explained Sage. "What can you tell me about Clinton Tate?"

"Ah, yes, the hotel owner," said Todd. "I guess he would be considered a suspect since the murder happened on his property, and he was involved in a business deal with the victim."

"That was my line of reasoning, too," confirmed Sage.

"Clinton moved to Clearwater about eight years ago," said Todd, "along with a slew of other big-money developers, looking to cash in on waterfront property. They were certainly a greedy lot, but I'm not aware of any scandals or serious conflicts involving any of Clinton's business deals."

"What about The Grand Hotel? Since Maybelle was planning to buy it from Clinton, could there have been any legal snafus regarding that transaction?"

"None that I know of," replied Todd. "He's selling off all his developments in Clearwater."

"Why?"

"I don't know the details, but there's a rumor circulating around town that he's planning to build a forty-million-dollar resort community in Costa Rica."

"He's leaving the country?"

"Apparently so. Maybe he wants to retire there. It's a beautiful place."

"Why hasn't he made any announcement about this development? That seems rather uncharacteristic for Clinton Tate."

"Yes," agreed Todd. "He's normally quite vocal about his accomplishments. I don't know why he's being so tight-lipped this time, unless he's still lining up his investors."

"He would need a whole bunch of them for a project that size—or a few with very deep pockets."

Todd nodded. "I'm sorry I don't have more information, but, for some reason, he's not ready to divulge any of the details."

"Actually, that's probably all the information I need on Clinton Tate. It sounds like he's just transferring his investments from domestic developments to international ones. There's nothing illegal about that. Thanks for your help, Todd."

As Sage was getting into her car, a blue sedan pulled up beside her. It was Murlene Wilson, a long-time friend of Ginger's. She came running over to give Sage a hug.

"I just couldn't believe the news about your mother," she exclaimed. "Has the Sheriff found out anything yet? How's your family holding up?"

"We're okay," replied Sage. "Unfortunately, the Sheriff hasn't heard anything from the kidnapper, but he thinks the abduction has something to do with Maybelle's murder."

"Really?" asked Murlene. "Poor Maybelle. I guess they haven't figured out yet who killed her?"

"No. My sisters and I are out today doing background checks on possible suspects."

Murlene's eyebrows rose in surprise. "That could be a pretty long list," she confided. "Maybelle was...well..."

"Pushy?" injected Sage.

"Very," she confirmed. "She felt it was her duty in life to tell other people how to run theirs. And she wasn't very tactful about it either."

"Is there anyone in particular you feel we should add to our list?"

"I assume Henry Jamison is on the list. That pathetic man; I don't know how he tolerated her all these years. I'll bet he thought about strangling her himself on more than one occasion. Of course, he's in Washington, D.C. most of the time now, since he's a Congressman."

"Yes. Curry is talking to his assistant today."

"Are there any women on your list?" asked Murlene. "I can think of about a dozen who've been tempted to put us all out of Maybelle's misery."

Sage smiled. "Actually there aren't, but if we don't turn up any good leads, I might get back to you about that possibility."

"Call me, dear. I want to help your mother any way I can."

Sage sat in her car, pondering what to do next. She had a nagging feeling that something just wasn't quite right about Clinton Tate's clandestine plans to move all his investments out of the country. Aware of his reputation for non-stop bragging about his self-made empire, this quiet transition was totally out of character for him. Perhaps a little more investigation was in order. She needed to concoct a scheme to gain access into Clinton Tate's inner sanctum, and talk to him face to face.

*   *   *   *   *   *   *   *   *   *

Cinnamon left the house shortly after Sage that morning. Being in the restaurant business and on her feet all day, business suits and heels weren't an option for her. Casual pants suits and cushy-soled shoes were her favored choice of clothing. She plopped her large leather handbag on the passenger seat in her red Jeep Cherokee and headed for the Clearwater Country Club to meet with Susan James, Kathy Freeman, and Belinda Cross—all members of Maybelle's favorite social committees. Yes, they had told her by phone this morning, they would be happy to "dish the dirt" on Maybelle Jamison. That wasn't actually the term they used, but it was accurate nonetheless.

Cinnamon turned into the country club's sweeping drive, leading up to the sprawling white stucco building. A young valet rushed to open the car door of her comparatively low-budget ride, trying to hide the smirk on his face. She watched him park her trusty red Jeep at the end of a long row of black Mercedes. In spite of their wealth, these people were so pathetically boring and predictable. Were they really so afraid to break their own self-imposed, socially-correct rules? How sad. Cinnamon firmly believed in creative self-expression—in all areas of her life.

The attendant at the front desk directed her out to the pool area, where she found the three chairladies ensconced at a table under the shade of a huge umbrella. The Clearwater Country Club boasts a gorgeous view of Pelican Bay; and on this cool, crisp March morning, with a clear blue sky overhead and the sun glinting off the water, Cinnamon savored the breathtaking scene.

As she approached the ladies' table, a waiter removed three champagne glasses and placed another Mimosa in front of each woman, along with a plate of dainty breakfast pastries. This should be interesting, thought Cinnamon, wondering if they were on round two or three. And it's only ten o'clock.

"Cinnamon," cried Susan. "I'm so sorry to hear about Ginger's abduction."

"Yes," added Kathy. "They're saying it might be the same person who killed Maybelle."

"This is all just so frightening," exclaimed Belinda. "Clearwater has always been such a quiet little town."

"It *is* scary," replied Cinnamon, taking the fourth seat at the table. "Thank you for meeting with me this morning."

"We wouldn't have it any other way," said Kathy. "How can we help?"

"Would you care for something to drink, dear, or a bite to eat?" asked Susan, pushing the plate of treats in Cinnamon's direction.

"Nothing to drink, thank you, but I'd love to sample something from your brunch tray," she replied, examining the beautifully displayed mini-scones and tiny quiches. Always on the look-out for new recipes and flavor combinations, Cinnamon never passed up an opportunity to test another chef's creations. She chose a taste-tempting sausage and spinach quiche and popped it into her mouth, nodding her approval.

"My sisters and I are making a list of possible suspects for Maybelle's murder," she said. "Have you heard about any conflicts or feuds involving Maybelle recently? Can you think of anyone who was angry enough to want her dead?"

The three ladies glanced at each other during an awkward pause. "Maybe not dead," replied Susan, taking a slug of champagne for courage, "just...gone."

"She was an absolute tyrant," added Belinda, twirling her glass nervously. "No one wanted to work with her."

"Especially after Clinton agreed to sell her the hotel," agreed Susan. "We were sick of her gloating. You'd think she was planning to purchase the entire town—not one silly little hotel."

"She wasn't gloating on Thursday," scoffed Kathy. "She was mad enough to spit nails!"

"You mean the day before she was murdered?" asked Cinnamon. "What happened?"

"She was angry with Clinton because he changed his mind about selling her the hotel. They had a knock-down-drag-out fight right here at the club and Clinton just stormed out."

"It was bizarre," added Belinda, downing the last of her drink. "Everyone knows he's selling off all his property to build some fancy multi-million dollar resort down in Costa Rica. Why didn't he want Maybelle's money?"

"Humph," groused Susan. "He didn't want money from any of us. My Frank asked him about becoming an investor in his new project, and he said it was a private deal—not open to other investors.

"He was sher-tain-ly glad to take our money when he first started his developments here in Clearwater," lisped Belinda, beginning to show the effects of her alcoholic beverage.

"He was groveling with both hands out," agreed Kathy, knocking back the last of her champagne and waving to the waiter for a refill. "Are you sure you don't want something to drink, dear?" she asked, followed by, "Hic".

"No thanks," replied Cinnamon. She had to speed up this interview before they all passed out. "Why did Clinton change his mind about selling the hotel to Maybelle?"

Kathy shrugged, her eyes beginning to blur.

Susan looked like the cat that swallowed the canary. "I know why," she smiled, waving her glass in the air.

"You don't," slurred Kathy.

"A little birdie told me," she hummed.

Cinnamon rubbed her temples, trying to ward off the tension headache creeping into her brain. "Why?" she pleaded.

"Yeah," asked Kathy. "Why?"

"Oh...I know," said Belinda, slowly rolling each word off her tangled tongue. "She told me she wasn't moving to that God forsaken jungle!"

"Who?" asked Cinnamon, impatiently.

"Marla, Clinton's wife," chuckled Susan. "She told him where he could put his fanzzy rezzort."

"You mean she's divorcing Clinton?"

Susan nodded, fading fast. "She gets to keep the hotel!"

Belinda cackled loudly at this revelation. "Where he could put it!" she giggled.

Cinnamon felt it was time to move on—these three were wasted. "Thanks, ladies. You've been very helpful."

They all saluted her with their champagne glasses, still giggling over Marla's revenge.

Cinnamon sat in her Jeep trying to piece together what she had gleaned from the "Mimosa Mamas".

Clinton Tate was selling all his property and moving to a foreign country where he had a major money deal already in place. He and Maybelle argued the day before she died, and his wife planned to divorce him and take part of his assets.

That doesn't sound like a motive for killing Maybelle, but Marla might want to watch her back."

* * * * * * * * * *

Before Sage could formulate her plan to invade Clinton Tate's headquarters, her cell phone rang. It was Cinnamon. "I just finished my interview with 'the ladies who lunch'," she said. "They decided to jump-start their day in 'Mimosaville'."

Sage chuckled. "Did you manage to find out anything important before they sailed?"

"Yeah, Clinton Tate is selling off all his property here in order to build a resort in Costa Rica; but there's a slight glitch in his plan."

"What do you mean? I heard about the resort, but not any problems associated with it."

"Well, that's because you didn't get it from the loose-lipped 'Mimosa Mamas'. His wife, Marla, decided she didn't want to move to...and I quote, 'That God forsaken jungle,' so she's divorcing Clinton and taking the hotel as part of her property settlement."

"He told Maybelle he couldn't sell her the hotel?"

"Yep, the day before she was murdered. They had a confrontation at the country club about it."

"Hmm," mused Sage. "Then he didn't really have a reason to kill her. But, it's odd that he's being so 'hush-hush' about this development in Costa Rica."

"And he's turned away several local investors. He told them the deal is private."

"Clinton Tate turning down money?" asked Sage. "What's wrong with that picture?"

"It sounded kind of fishy to me, too, but I don't know how we could check it out. Where do we go from here?"

"I was planning to talk to Clinton, but that's probably a waste of time," replied Sage.

"I think I'll head over to the hotel and check in with Pepper," said Cinnamon.

"Okay. I'll see if Curry found out anything at Henry Jamison's office."

Sage started her car, planning to stop by the house to check on Mace, and then call Curry for an update on her interview. As she pulled out of the parking lot, she noticed a man wearing dark sunglasses, sitting in a black sedan, which was parked across the street. He was staring directly at her. Her internal warning system kicked in, causing the hair on the back of her neck to stand up. She shook it off, dismissing the feeling. This is ridiculous, she thought, I'm just spooked because of this murder and kidnapping.

She pulled out onto the street, but couldn't resist glancing in her rear view mirror just in time to see the sedan pull out into traffic a couple of cars behind her. Purely coincidence, she told herself; but her hands tightened slightly around the steering wheel.

She turned right onto Harbor Drive, still heading for home, but the sedan turned right, too, staying one or two cars behind her. "Okay—change of plans," she said, as her heart began to pound faster. It was time to test her theory of coincidence. Sage maintained her speed, but turned left onto the next street, then right just one block later. The sedan followed suit.

"Not a good sign," she admitted. She couldn't allow this stalker to follow her home, where Mace was waiting. She needed to find a public place to go. The most obvious choice was the Sheriff's office—surely she would be safe there.

Once again, she turned onto Harbor Drive, a new five-lane highway running east and west through the main business district in Clearwater. Zipping along at 50 miles per hour, Sage watched the oncoming traffic, hopping to make a quick left turn through an opening. It was a last-ditch effort to try to lose this creep.

She spotted a narrow space in the line of traffic and whipped the steering wheel sharply to the left, narrowly missing

45

the front bumper of an oncoming vehicle. The irate driver blasted her with his horn. The black sedan quickly pulled into the turning lane, but couldn't get through the solid line of traffic.

"Yes!" cried Sage, elated over her small victory, but still trembling with fear. She took a deep breath, trying to calm herself. Why the hell was someone following her? Maybelle was dead, taking whatever secrets she had along with her; and Ginger's kidnapper would certainly know how to get in touch with her family. What did this guy want from her?

After returning from her temporary reverie, she glanced in the mirror again. The stalker was back on her tail—just two cars back.

"Shit!" she cried, stomping on the accelerator. "Okay, scumbag. If you want to follow me, go ahead. I'm plowing right through the front door of the Morgan County Sherriff's Office." And that is exactly what she did. Well—almost. She bounced up over the side walk and stopped short of the brick wall, narrowly missing an unsuspecting deputy coming out of the building. Her goal was to attract attention, and she got it in spades.

The driver in the black sedan stared at her as he drove by, and then turned off at the first intersection, disappearing into the traffic. Damn, she was so shaken by the ordeal, she hadn't thought to look at his license plate numbers.

"Sage," cried Jason, running up to her car. "What the hell are you doing?"

She closed her eyes and mentally banged her head on the steering wheel. Why was this happening? She desperately wanted her life back to normal again—no more murder, no more kidnapping, and no more frantic car chases. Enough already!

Jason, sensing her distress opened the car door and gently helped her out.

* * * * * * * * * *

"Did you get his license plate number?" he asked, after planting her on a chair in his office. He was baffled by her report of the car-chase incident. Could it have something to do with Maybelle's murder? It just didn't make any sense.

"No," she replied wearily. "He stayed one or two cars behind me the whole time. And I was too upset after crashing into the sidewalk to think about it."

"Why would someone chase you? Do you think it's related to a case you're working on now? You've defended some dangerous characters in the past."

Sage glared at him. "Don't pull that moral crap on me," she sneered. "It's not my fault our Justice System is in shambles. I'm doing my best to draw attention to all the glaring loop-holes every time I use them to keep one of my clients out of jail, but it's up to the law makers to fix the problem. I can't fix it and you can't fix it and our honorable elected officials can't seem to get their act together long enough to fix it."

"That's not what I was implying," countered Jason, trying to calm her down. "I meant someone who's trying to stall the investigation process for one of your clients."

Sage paused, sorting through the details of all her open cases. "No. I'm not working on any criminal cases right now. The worst scenario I'm dealing with is a super-rich, elderly couple in the throws of divorce; dead-locked in a vicious custody battle over their pet Chihuahua, Skippy."

Jason chuckled. She never ceased to amaze him. Her life was one big roller coaster ride, and he planned to hang on tight. But he didn't like the direction this case was heading; first murder, then kidnapping and now car chases. There seemed to be a nasty pattern developing here. Could all these events be related?

Chapter Six

Curry was next to leave the McCormick house that morning. She glided out to her sporty blue Miata, her long brunette tresses blowing gently in the cool March breeze. She and Pepper were walking advertisements for their trendy fashion designs. She gracefully folded her long, shapely legs into the compact vehicle, placed her tiny designer handbag on the passenger seat, and headed for Congressman Henry Jamison's office to talk to his assistant, Sharon Daniels.

Sharon was obsessed with fashion and counted on Curry and Pepper to keep her on the cutting edge. As the spokesperson for a local congressman and often in the public eye, she was quite conscious about her professional image. Since the McCormick twins were also her friends, Sharon was thrilled to help investigate Ginger's kidnapping, as well as Maybelle's murder.

The Congressman's office was located in Clearwater's original business district. Now called "Old Towne", it consisted of a four-block area of quaint shops, built in the early 1900's. All the buildings were beautifully restored, and the area was a highly desirable retail location, packed with trendy shops and eclectic cafes.

"Sharon," said Curry, "thank you so much for meeting with me. I know you must be swamped with phone calls about the Congressman's wife."

"It's been crazy around here. We're working overtime today. Our office is usually closed on Saturday," she said, directing Curry into her office. "Hold my calls, please, Annette," she told her secretary, as she closed the office door.

"How is your family holding up? The Sheriff doesn't have any leads about your mother's kidnapper?" she asked.

"Not yet," replied Curry. "My sisters and I are doing some investigating on our own. I know this is awkward for you, since the Congressman is your boss, but could he possibly be involved in Maybelle's death?"

"Off-hand," replied Sharon, "I would say no. I've only worked for him about eight months now, and he has been extremely stressed out, but not because of Maybelle."

"Why?" asked Curry.

"Henry Jamison has been a U.S. Representative for fifteen years. When he was first elected, he expected to keep moving up the political ladder; but apparently, it just wasn't in the cards for him. He's had a rather lackluster career. Then, after the scandal three years ago, about the adulterous affair he had with his assistant in Washington, he never overcame the backlash from his constituents or the party leaders.

"Needless to say, it didn't do much to improve his marriage relationship either," she continued. "But Maybelle was remarkably unfazed by the scandal. She just carried on as if nothing had happened. I don't know if that was an act to hide her true feelings or if she really didn't care. In any case, she aced the role of the perfect politician's wife."

"From what I've heard about Maybelle," said Curry, "it probably wasn't an act. She had her own agenda, and everybody else was just an expendable 'extra'. As long as she had money and social status, and no one was preventing her from getting what she wanted, she was happy as a clam."

"That about sums it up," agreed Sharon. "Unfortunately, the party has asked Henry to give up his seat for a rising young star they plan to groom for a higher office. He was already depressed over the fact that his career was stagnant, but he went ballistic over the news that he's being 'put out to pasture' by the party."

"I can see why," said Curry.

"It's odd, though," added Sharon. "The last few months, he seemed to be fairly content with the whole situation. I don't know what happened to change his attitude, but he's actually been rather cheerful. At least until Maybelle was murdered. The only communication I've received from him since yesterday is that his plane will be arriving at four o'clock this afternoon. I'm sending an aide to pick him up at the airport. Maybelle's funeral is scheduled for Monday."

"This murder has everyone baffled," said Curry. "We thought we had a viable suspect, but it turns out he has an alibi for the time of the murder. We're running out of leads."

"I wish I could be more helpful. I know how worried you must be about your mother."

Curry nodded. "We'll just have to keep searching. Thanks for your time, Sharon." Disappointed that her mission hadn't been more productive, she walked outside and sat down on one of the wooden benches strategically placed along the wide brick sidewalks for weary shoppers to rest. It was a glorious, sunny spring day, with a gentle breeze blowing in off the bay. She closed her eyes for a moment, feeling the warmth of the sun on her face and listening to the calls of the seagulls gliding overhead.

Life in a small town certainly moved at a more civilized pace. She loved her design career and running the boutique, but life in Houston was hectic. Maybe she should talk to Pepper about the possibility of moving their business to Clearwater—after they got Mother back. And they would!

Curry pulled out her cell phone and called Sage. "Have you found any more leads?"

"No," replied Sage, "but I'm beginning to think this murder/kidnapping scenario is bigger than Glen Durst." While sitting in the lobby of the Sheriff's office, Sage told Curry about the mysterious man who chased her by car. "Jason is trying to convince me that it was related to one of my criminal cases, but my gut tells me otherwise."

"Who do you think it could be?"

"I don't know, but murder, kidnapping and stalking are beginning to add up to some type of organized activity by my way of thinking. Did you find out anything at Henry Jamison's office?"

"Not a motive for murdering Maybelle, but the Congressman is about to be out of a job. His party has asked him to give up his seat for someone younger and more promotable."

"Good grief," said Sage. "After fifteen years, they've just decided to toss him out? How's he handling it?"

"Sharon said, at first he was angry, but now he seems perfectly content with the whole situation. Maybe he's decided to start a new career."

"I guess he doesn't have much choice."

"What should I do now?" asked Curry.

"I'm fresh out of ideas," replied Sage. "Cinnamon is going over to check on Pepper. So far they haven't turned up anything either, other than the fact that Clinton Tate changed his mind about selling the hotel to Maybelle. Apparently it's going to his wife, Marla, as part of their divorce settlement."

"Bummer," replied Curry. "Does that mean he's off the suspect list?"

"I think so," confirmed Sage.

"I guess I'll go back to the house then, because I don't have a clue where to look next." As Curry hung up the phone, she heard someone calling her name. She looked up to see Mary Ann Parker waving at her from the shop across the street.

Mary Ann, an old family friend, owned an antique shop in Old Towne. As a child, Curry loved browsing through the beautiful furniture and accessories that filled the retail space. Mary Ann was a talented interior designer with a good eye for quality. Curry walked across the street, greeting her with a warm hug.

"Have you found out anything about your mother yet?" asked Mary Ann. "This whole business is such a nightmare, with Maybelle's murder and Ginger's kidnapping. I just can't believe it."

"We haven't heard anything so far," replied Curry. "We're doing everything we can to track down leads."

"That Maybelle," exclaimed Mary Ann. "If she just hadn't been such a bully, she might still be alive. And poor Ginger would be safe."

"What do you mean?" asked Curry.

"Well, don't you think she was killed because of her obsession over that hotel? She was in here on Thursday morning, making plans to redecorate the owner's residence on the fourth floor. She was planning to live there and run the hotel herself. All she could talk about was how she was going to clean house and sweep out the riff-raff."

"Are you talking about Glen Durst, the hotel manager?"

"Apparently the head chef, too. She said she was going to talk to Cinnamon about taking over the restaurant."

"Maybelle was going to replace Gordon Ellis, too?"

"That's what she said."

"I wonder why he didn't mention it to Cinnamon yesterday?"

"Perhaps Maybelle hadn't told him yet, because Thursday evening she found out that Clinton Tate changed his mind about selling her the hotel. I would love to have been at the club to see that showdown."

"If she found out Thursday night that she couldn't buy the hotel, why did she go there Friday morning?"

"Obviously, you don't know Maybelle very well. She doesn't take 'no' for an answer. When she decides she wants something—come hell or high water—she's going to get it."

"I guess she tried to bully the wrong person," said Curry. "The question is: Who?"

"That's what we're all asking," agreed Mary Ann.

Curry watched as Sharon came out of Congressman Jamison's office and waved at her.

"Curry," she called. "I need to ask you something."

Just as Sharon stepped off the sidewalk to cross the street, the windows in the office exploded with a deafening roar. Her body sailed through the air and landed a few feet from Curry and Mary Ann, who were knocked backwards onto the sidewalk with the force of the explosion. Searing flames and black smoke rose from the office roof, which was blown into a million pieces and rained down on the street as frightened pedestrians ran screaming for safety.

Dazed by the blast, Curry had temporarily lost her hearing, but was uninjured other than a few tiny cuts from the flying glass. "Call 911!" she screamed at Mary Ann, who was still sitting in shock on the sidewalk.

Mary Ann crawled up the steps to her shop to make the call. Curry ran over to check on Sharon, who lay in a heap on the sidewalk. She was alive, but unconscious. Curry was afraid to move her without knowing how severe her injuries were.

Feeling helpless, she collapsed onto the sidewalk beside Sharon to wait for the ambulances and fire trucks to arrive. She could already hear the sirens in the distance. That emergency switchboard was probably lit up like a Christmas tree. News in a small town like Clearwater travels fast. Hell, this town was so small they probably heard the explosion at the call center.

What on earth happened, she wondered, as she stared across the street at the orange and red flames leaping into the sky? Did a gas line explode, or was it...a bomb?

* * * * * * * * * *

At the Sheriff's Department, a deputy came running into Jason's office. "There's been an explosion at Henry Jamison's office," he cried. "We've got a real mess in Old Towne."

Jason jumped up from his desk and ran out into the hall. Sage, who was just leaving the building, turned to face him when she heard the deputy's announcement.

"Oh, my God! Curry," she cried. "She just left the Congressman's office."

"Get in," Jason ordered, motioning to his vehicle, as they ran out into the parking lot.

They arrived at the chaotic scene in eight minutes flat. It's amazing the affect those sirens and flashing lights have on traffic. Sage quickly scanned the debris-covered scene and spotted Curry sitting on the sidewalk next to Sharon Daniels. Several ambulances were on the scene, and a couple of paramedics were checking Sharon's injuries, but Curry appeared to be all right.

"Curry!" yelled Sage, running toward her sister and hugging her, as a fireman placed a blanket around her shoulders. Curry was trembling from fear and the shock of the explosion.

"What happened?" asked Sage.

"I don't know. I was talking to Mary Ann out here on the sidewalk, and Sharon was crossing the street to talk to me when the whole damned building exploded."

"You mean...like a bomb?"

"That's what it looked like, but I guess it could have been a gas line."

"I'm just glad you're okay," said Sage.

The two sisters watched as the paramedics loaded Sharon into one of the ambulances and headed for the hospital. Her injuries were severe, but at least she should survive. They stared at the mass destruction surrounding them, as the firemen worked frantically to douse the flames and stop the fire from spreading to the adjacent shops.

"My car," whimpered Curry, gazing at the charred, crumpled mass of metal parked directly in front of the Congressman's office.

"Just be very thankful that you weren't in it," replied Sage.

Curry began to cry, overwhelmed by the traumatic event, as well as her own narrow escape from death.

Sage tried to comfort her sister, as her analytical brain started shuffling the parts of this puzzle. She was positive now that this crime spree was not linked to Glen Durst. It also had nothing to do with her criminal cases. There was something more sinister at work here, and she intended to find out what it was.

The remaining paramedic team cleaned and bandaged Curry's minor cuts. She assured them that she was fine and didn't need to go to the hospital. After that, the two sisters sat on a bench, watching silently as the firefighters put out the fire.

Since they had no transportation, they decided to wait for Jason's report on the explosion. Sage dared not call Mace. He had enough to worry about without adding Curry's near-death accident to the mix. Pepper and Cinnamon were working on the investigation at the hotel; there was nothing they could do here. So the two sisters sat and waited—not knowing what else to do.

The coroner arrived on the scene and hauled two victims out of the rubble that was once Congressman Jamison's office. The building was almost completely demolished. Sage shivered at the sight of the black body bags. There would have been three bodies if Sharon hadn't stepped out of the office to talk to Curry, or four if Curry had lingered there much longer. She didn't want to think about that possibility.

* * * * * * * * * *

The Fire Chief and Jason scoured what was left of the charred building, looking for the source of the explosion.

"Here," said the chief, pointing to the area at the back of the building that once housed the kitchen. "It was definitely a bomb. Our lab will need to investigate to determine the type, but it looks like plastic explosives on a timer."

Jason shook his head in disbelief, "Why would someone blow up the Congressman's office? He wasn't even here."

"Maybe they didn't know that," said the Chief. "Or maybe it wasn't meant to kill him—just scare him. His office is normally closed on weekends."

"I think they made their point," replied Jason. "Jamison's daughter has already called him to report the explosion. He's at the airport in Washington now, but his plane gets in here at four o'clock, and my deputies will be there to pick him up at the airport. We're going to have a long chat with the Congressman."

On his way back to his vehicle, Jason spotted Sage and Curry sitting on the bench across the street. He was so busy coordinating the rescue and clean-up efforts of the firemen, deputies and paramedics, he had forgotten about the two women.

"I'm sorry, Sage. I didn't know you were still here. I assumed you had called someone to take you home. Are you okay Curry?"

"I'm fine," she replied.

"We wanted to wait and get the official report about the explosion," said Sage.

Jason paused. He knew now that her instincts were right. This series of crimes involved more than one simple murder. "It was a bomb," he said.

"Now do you believe that man wasn't stalking me because of one of my criminal cases?" asked Sage. "This is something big, Jason. This is evil—it's powerful, and it's obviously well-planned."

"And it's got something to do with the Congressman," added Jason. "We're picking him up this afternoon at the airport. If he won't talk to us, I'm calling in the F.B.I."

Sage blinked. "Do you think it could be an international incident? Are you talking about terrorists in Clearwater?"

Sage and Curry stared at him in horror. It had never occurred to either of them that their mother might have been kidnapped by terrorists. That stuff happens in foreign countries, not America, and definitely not in little towns like Clearwater.

"I'm going to wait and see what Henry Jamison has to say. Some wacko constituent, pissed off with the government could have caused this explosion. They know how to make bombs in this country, too, you know. But this string of crimes has got me baffled. I may have to call for back-up if I don't get some answers soon."

Sage nodded. She understood his frustration, because she felt the same way. Their once quiet little community was under siege by some unknown evil force that felt like they were in the middle of a war zone. How do you stop something you can't even see? Her fighting spirit was beginning to sag. She was fresh out of ideas.

Sage sighed, trying desperately to hold on to a glimmer of hope, "Can you take us back to your office to get my car?"

"Sure. We can leave now."

On the way back to the Sheriff's office, Sage dialed Cinnamon's cell phone. She wanted to let her sisters know that Curry was all right, just in case they heard about the explosion. But Cinnamon didn't answer, and the call was directed to her voice mail. That's strange, Sage thought. She left a message telling Cinnamon that she and Curry would be at the house if she needed them.

"She didn't answer?" asked Curry. "Maybe her phone battery is dead. Try Pepper."

Sage dialed Pepper's cell phone with the same results.

"What's wrong?" asked Jason.

"Cinnamon and Pepper aren't answering their phones," replied Sage. "They're supposed to be at the hotel."

"Do you want me to send a deputy over there to check on them?"

"No," replied Sage. "You've got your hands full dealing with this explosion and Henry Jamison. I'll drop Curry off at the house and check on them myself."

Curry started to protest, but she was beginning to feel the aftershock of the bomb blast. She desperately needed to soak in a hot bath and rest.

"Oh," she said, "in all the mayhem, I forgot to tell you. Mary Ann said Maybelle was in her shop Thursday morning and mentioned that she was not only planning to fire Glen but Gordon as well."

"The chef?" asked Sage, looking at Jason. "Did you question Gordon Ellis yesterday?"

"Of course. I questioned all the hotel employees. Gordon Ellis was in a meeting with Jenny Hall, the event planner, at the time of Maybelle's murder."

"And getting fired is rarely a motive for murder," added Sage.

"Firing them wasn't exactly how Maybelle described it," said Curry, trying to remember Mary Ann's words. "She said she was cleaning house—getting rid of the 'riff-raff'.

"I wonder what she meant by that?" asked Jason.

"I don't know," replied Sage, "unless, like Glen Durst, Gordon Ellis isn't who he says he is."

Chapter Seven

Mace McCormick paced nervously across the family room floor in his two-story Victorian home on Lighthouse Drive. How could this be happening? His beloved wife of thirty-four years was nearly killed in a freak accident and, as if that wasn't bad enough, now someone had kidnapped her!

The Sheriff asked him to stay home in case the kidnappers called, but he knew in his heart that just wasn't going to happen. Ginger wasn't kidnapped for a ransom; she was taken by the same person who killed Maybelle Jamison. Obviously, the killer thought Maybelle told Ginger something that could incriminate him. Mace was worried sick that Ginger would be killed, too; and he felt helpless to stop it.

What on earth had Maybelle done this time to cause such a disaster? She had always been self-centered and domineering. Mace learned that fact early on in their two-year marriage. Nothing he did could make her happy—she always wanted more. Her aggressive behavior offended almost everyone who came in contact with her, but most people simply avoided her. He wasn't aware of anyone angry enough to kill her. She must have gotten mixed up with something really evil to stir up this much trouble.

Mace glanced out the front window and waved at Deputy Sam Davis, sitting in a cruiser parked at the curb. Jason had assigned him to watch the house in case the kidnapper showed up. Fat chance! He already had Ginger. Why would he come here? Mace began to pace again, raking his hands fretfully through his short, sandy-blonde hair. Waiting around here was just a waste of time. He should be out there looking for Ginger, like his four daughters were at this very moment. At least they were doing something productive. He wasn't doing anything but wearing a deeper path in the already worn family room carpet.

But, where would he go to look for Ginger? Since no one knew why Maybelle was killed in the first place, how would they know where to find her killer? Sage was checking on Clinton Tate, Curry was talking to Henry Jamison's assistant, Cinnamon was questioning Maybelle's acquaintances, and Pepper was interviewing the hotel employees again. Who was left?

If Maybelle was blackmailing Glen Durst, then maybe she was threatening to expose someone else—someone with a secret so evil he was willing to kill in order to keep it hidden. But who could that be? And what was he trying to hide? Before yesterday, Mace never would have imagined that such a wicked and destructive person could be lurking in Clearwater. But it was all too real today, and someone had to stop him before anyone else was hurt.

Mace grabbed a pen and pad from the desk and plopped down in one of the upholstered chairs in the family room. He began to jot down the names of possible suspects and motives. It helped him to think more clearly when he could see things laid out neatly in a diagram format. It was part of his training as an engineer to organize information into patterns. He was deep in thought, sketching frantically, when he heard the kitchen door lock click.

He raised his head to listen, thinking one of the girls must have returned, desperately hoping they had good news about Ginger. But before he could get up from the chair, he felt the cold metal barrel of a gun pressed against the back of his neck. Mace froze in terror.

"Don't move," ordered an unfamiliar, deep, male voice.

Mace didn't know much about guns, in spite of the fact that he was born and raised in Texas, but he knew which end of a gun could cause the most damage, so he was more than willing to oblige.

"Where is she?" demanded the intruder.

Mace was completely baffled by this new turn of events. Who the hell is this guy, he thought? Is he Ginger's kidnapper? If he already has Ginger, then who is he looking for? Come to think of it, where the hell is that deputy who's supposed to be guarding the house?

"Who?" asked Mace.

"Your wife, you moron. Where did they take her?"

"What are you talking about?" asked Mace, thoroughly confused. "She was kidnapped from the hospital, and we don't know where she is. We think Maybelle Jamison's killer took her."

The stranger stepped in front of Mace, pointing the gun at his forehead. He wore a black sweatshirt and black pants, with a ski mask pulled over his head. Only his dark brown eyes were visible, as he stared at Mace, trying to gauge his sincerity. "We didn't take your wife from the hospital," he replied. "Someone else got to her first. They were keeping her at the hotel, but when our attempt to kill her failed, they moved her to another location."

Mace turned pale when he heard this news. They had tried to kill Ginger? Oh, my God! Was she already dead? No! He refused to believe it. It couldn't be true. He had to do something—he needed to alert the deputy. But how?

"Stand up," said the man, motioning with his pistol.

Mace rose from the chair, hoping to get closer to the window where the deputy might see him. "Who took Ginger from the hospital?" he asked, backing up slowly towards the window.

But the intruder shoved him in the direction of the kitchen. "We don't know," he said. "We thought it was the Sheriff, trying to protect her. Isn't that why a deputy's car is sitting out front?"

"The Sheriff doesn't know where she is. He thinks she was kidnapped by Maybelle's killer," replied Mace,

"That was the plan," sneered the stranger. "That Jamison bitch was sticking her nose in where it didn't belong, so we had to take her out before she caused any more trouble. But she passed along some damaging information to your wife before she died."

"Ginger didn't hear Maybelle say anything," argued Mace. "She told the Sheriff everything that happened at the hotel that morning. Then she was kidnapped from the hospital a few hours later. The Sheriff didn't take her. She's not here at the house. You said she was taken to the hotel, and now you think her kidnapper has moved her to another location. If you don't have her, then who does?"

"You'd better not be lying to me," exclaimed the man, becoming increasingly agitated, "or I'll blow your damned head off! If it's not the Sheriff, then it could be the F.B.I. and that's bad news." He glanced around the room nervously, and then backed up toward the hallway leading to the bedrooms. "Down there," he ordered, motioning for Mace to move.

"I'm telling you," Mace yelled. "Ginger is not here! No one is here but me and that deputy out front!"

"I plan to check that out for myself," countered the stranger. "Now move!"

Mace walked slowly down the hallway and into the master bedroom. The gunman quickly scanned the area, checking the bathroom and closet. Satisfied that the room was empty, they moved on to the second bedroom, with the same results.

"Upstairs," he said, giving Mace another shove.

They headed back down the hallway. Where is that damned deputy, thought Mace?

As Mace reached the entry hall and stepped up onto the staircase, they heard a loud "boom" in the distance that rattled every window in the house. Temporarily startled by the explosion, the intruder turned away briefly. Mace took advantage of the moment and slapped the gun from his hand.

It went flying across the room and bounced underneath one of the upholstered chairs. Mace slammed the stranger against the wall and made a dash for the front door. He barely managed to get it open when the man grabbed him around the neck, attempting to pull him back inside.

When Deputy Davis witnessed this commotion, he jumped out of his cruiser to join the melee, running through the doorway and making a flying leap at the intruder. It was a valiant effort; unfortunately, the man caught a glimpse of the movement and turned to the side just in time to avoid being hit. Deputy Davis did a belly flop on the family room rug, landing with a violent thud, and lay sprawled face down on the floor. But his action wasn't a total loss. It distracted the intruder long enough for Mace to give him a powerful shove from behind, sending him stumbling over the prostrate deputy.

The series of events looked like a scene from the "Keystone Kops", and would have been quite comical if it weren't so real and downright dangerous. At least the gun was now out of reach.

The stunned deputy rolled over to grab the stranger, who wriggled and kicked to avoid capture. He jumped up to run, but

Mace tackled him to the floor, trying to hold onto the frantic man's legs, while Deputy Davis scrambled over to help.

In desperation, the man finally kicked himself free and dashed out the back door, as Mace and Deputy Davis sat staring at each other in baffled silence.

"What the hell was that noise?" asked Mace.

"Who the hell was that man?" asked Deputy Davis.

The two men, both well-past middle-age and still breathing hard from their terrifying scuffle, collapsed into the chairs in the family room. Mace gave his statement to the Deputy about the intruder.

"He, or one of his partners, killed Maybelle," said Mace. "And they were planning to kill Ginger, too, but someone else took her from the hospital before they had the chance. The man who broke in thought it was the Sheriff, but I told him it wasn't. Then he said it might be the F.B.I., and he was really worried about that idea. Do you think there could be some kind of terrorist group in Clearwater, and the F.B.I. is here watching them?"

"As far as I know, the F.B.I. hasn't notified the Sheriff's office that they're investigating anyone here, but that doesn't mean they're not. They don't always keep the local law enforcement informed, especially if it's some kind of undercover investigation."

"I guess Jason needs to find out, before this group attacks someone else," suggested Mace. "How on earth did Maybelle get involved in something like that? She usually hangs out with the country club set—not terrorists."

"Your guess is as good as mine," replied Deputy Davis. "She does like to meddle in other people's business and isn't shy about criticizing the local law enforcement. I know that from personal experience, especially when her husband was mayor."

"Tell me about it," said Mace, remembering the unrelenting complaints he endured during his marriage to Maybelle. He was lucky to escape with his self-esteem mostly intact. And then he met Ginger, the love of his life. Her gentle and caring personality was the complete opposite of Maybelle's.

"Did the guy who broke in have a gun?" asked Deputy Davis.

"Yeah," said Mace. "It bounced underneath that chair when he dropped it. I'm sure there are fingerprints on it. He wasn't wearing any gloves. I guess he wasn't as smart as he thought."

The deputy carefully moved the large upholstered chair, and spotted the gun. He glanced at Mace excitedly, "Those fingerprints could be the first clue we've found in this case. If they're on file, we'll nail him. He could lead us to the rest of his group, too. Did he say why they killed Maybelle?"

"No," replied Mace. "Just that she stuck her nose in where it didn't belong and found out about something they didn't want her to expose."

"I guess she finally ruffled the wrong feathers," said the deputy.

"Apparently so," agreed Mace.

"I'll take this evidence down to the office and turn in my report to the Sheriff. I'm sure he'll want to check with the F.B.I. field office to see if that lunatic was right about them taking Ginger. He said she was at the hotel?"

"Yeah," confirmed Mace. "But he and his group found out where she was and tried to kill her, so he assumed her kidnapper had moved her to another location. I hope that means she's safe now. I'd much rather think the F.B.I. has her instead of Maybelle's killer."

"A bunch of criminals running around killing people right here in Clearwater," said the deputy, shaking his head in disbelief. "I wonder what they're trying to cover up? Drugs maybe? Or weapons?"

Mace shrugged. "It's scary. I sure hope Jason can get all this straightened out. Did you find out yet what that explosion noise was about?"

"A building exploded in Old Towne. The Sheriff is there now investigating. I heard it was Congressman Jamison's office."

"Jamison?" repeated Mace. "Do you think this group is after him, too?" He paused for a moment, thinking. "Oh, my God!" he cried suddenly. "Curry was supposed to go to Jamison's office this morning to talk to his assistant."

The deputy stared at him with a blank look on his face. "I can find out if anyone was hurt. I'm sure the Sheriff would have called you by now if Curry was injured," he added, trying to reassure Mace, and pulling out his radio.

Mace listed intently to the crackling noise of the deputy's radio, while he tried to contact someone at the scene of the explosion.

"This is Deputy Pearson," said a voice finally.

"Were there any injuries in the office explosion?" asked Deputy Davis.

"Two employees are dead. The assistant was taken to the hospital in critical condition," replied Deputy Pearson.

"Oh, my God," said Mace. "These people really are terrorists. How many more innocent victims are going to die before they're stopped?"

The deputy couldn't answer that question. Their once quiet little community was beginning to feel like the front lines of a battle field.

Relieved to hear that Curry was all right, and somewhat comforted by the thought that the F.B.I. might be protecting Ginger from the assassins, Mace collapsed into the nearest chair, exhausted from the day's excitement.

"I'll have the Sheriff call you when he's finished at the explosion scene," offered Deputy Davis.

Mace just nodded and closed his eyes. He couldn't deal with any more trauma at the moment. After he rested for a while, he would call all his daughters to check on them and pass along the good news about Ginger—a least he hoped it was good news—he really didn't have any proof that she was safe in the protective custody of the F.B.I. But he wanted to believe that she was.

A short while later, Sage and Curry came in the back door. They were concerned when they saw Mace slumped in the chair.

"What's wrong?" asked Sage. "Did you hear something about Mother?"

Mace looked up, noticing Curry's bandages. "Are you okay?" he asked. "We heard the explosion and Deputy Davis called the scene to find out if you'd been hurt."

"I'm fine," answered Curry. "Just a few cuts."

"I had a rather exciting morning, too," said Mace. "Maybelle's killer stopped by for a chat."

"What?" screeched Sage. "Why would he come here? Was he trying to hurt you? Where is he? What happened?"

"He was looking for your mother," smiled Mace. "His group didn't kidnap her from the hospital. They were planning to kill her, but someone else nabbed her before they could do it. The man who broke in this morning thought it was the Sheriff, but I told him Jason doesn't know where Ginger is. So, he decided it must be the F.B.I."

"The F.B.I.?" asked Curry. "He thinks the F.B.I. has her? That's good news, isn't it?"

"Deputy Davis couldn't confirm it. He said Jason would call them when he got back from the explosion scene. But it's a better scenario than thinking Ginger is with the killers."

"That's for sure," added Sage. "What happened to the killer? Did he get away?"

"Yeah," said Mace. "But I managed to get his gun away from him. The Sheriff's office will check it for prints. Hopefully this guy has a record and the officers can match his prints."

"Then we would know who killed Maybelle," added Curry.

"Perhaps," agreed Sage. "Why would the F.B.I. be here in Clearwater? This group must be into some kind of international crime. That's not good."

"I know," said Mace. "We'll have to wait and hear what Jason has to say. The guy who broke into the house said the kidnappers were holding Ginger at The Grand Hotel, but he thought they had moved her to another location."

"Mother is at the hotel?" asked Curry.

"She was at first," he corrected. "She might be somewhere else by now."

"We need to tell Cinnamon and Pepper," said Curry. "They're at the hotel now."

"Call them," said Mace.

"We already tried to call them, but they didn't answer," replied Sage. "I was planning to go there after I dropped Curry off at the house. She needs to change clothes and rest a while after her explosion ordeal."

"I'll go to the hotel," offered Mace. "You've been out all day."

"It might be best if you stayed here with Curry, in case the terrorists decide to drop by again. Is the deputy coming back?"

Curry glanced at Mace. "Maybe we should all go to the hotel. I'm not up for anymore terrorist visits."

Their nerves were so frazzled, they nearly jumped out of their skins when the doorbell rang.

Chapter Eight

After Cinnamon reported to Sage about her interview with the ladies at the country club, she drove to The Grand Hotel to check on Pepper's progress.

All morning long, Pepper had been hounding every employee who would stop long enough to talk to her about Maybelle's murder. She was getting nowhere fast, and her Ferragamo heels were taking their toll on her tired, sore feet. She plopped down in one of the cushy leather chairs in the lobby and kicked off her shoes. This is a waste of time she thought impatiently, as she leaned back and closed her weary eyes. No one saw anything and no one heard anything.

The elevator bell dinged and the doors slid open. Pepper watched as a young man, dressed in a dark business suit walked hurriedly through the lobby. A man on a mission, she thought, scanning him from head to toe. It was part of her nature, as well as her talent as a designer, to notice details. The man had an earpiece in his left ear with a wire running down underneath his collar, and he was talking—with no one in sight. "He's wired," she said, sitting up straight in her chair. Why would someone be wearing such a device? Could he be a body guard? Was someone famous staying at the hotel? In Clearwater? Not likely.

Pepper slipped on her shoes and scampered after her new target. Her heart raced with fear as she sneaked along behind him, praying that her curiosity wouldn't put her in grave danger. She had no idea who he was or where he was going, but she intended to find out—one way or another.

After her boring and nonproductive morning interview session with the hotel employees, she now tingled with the excitement of the chase. This espionage stuff could get addictive she thought, feeling the rush of adrenaline—as long as you don't get caught, that is.

Pepper watched intently from behind a large potted plant, as the man unlocked the door to a storage room and slipped inside. Now what? Should she take a peek inside or wait? Finally, she stepped out from her hiding place to approach the door, when it swung open and the man came out, carrying a briefcase. She gasped and nearly tripped over her own feet as she lunged back into hiding.

The man scurried down the hallway, just in time to catch the elevator. Pepper watched, as he pulled a key from his pocket and inserted it into the elevator controls. He was going up to the fourth floor. The elevator only went up to the third floor unless you used a key—it was a private area.

Hmm, she mused, there must be someone important here to rate the V.I.P. treatment on level four, not to mention the fact that they needed a body guard. Is that what he was? Even after her heart-stopping, clandestine surveillance, she still didn't have a clue.

* * * * * * * * * *

Up on the fourth floor, Ginger was restless. Even with the sedative the doctor had given her last night after her near-drowning episode, she had slept fitfully. She was determined to get out of this place—terrorists or no terrorists.

Every time one of the F.B.I. agents opened the door to her room, she did her best to peek outside into the hallway, trying to get a feel for the guard arrangement. By her calculation, there were only three agents: that nice young man, Peter Dalton, who was in charge of this operation and his two assistants, Ted Johnson and Harriet Blair.

Ted usually stood guard by the elevator door and Harriet relieved him occasionally. Peter brought Ginger's meals, but he hadn't talked much since she told him about hearing the name "Applewhite." She didn't know why that name had touched such a nerve, but Peter flew out of here like a whirlwind, and he hadn't questioned her since. Her only goal now was to get out of this place any way she could.

70

She dismissed the idea of trying to sneak up on Ted at the elevator, knock him out and take the elevator down to the first floor. Even if she could manage to overpower him, which was a stretch, she doubted if she could get her door unlocked without him hearing her.

It was too bad her food trays weren't being delivered by the kitchen staff, or she could slip a note under a lettuce leaf asking Gordon, the chef, to contact Cinnamon. Even an S.O.S. spelled out in croutons would suffice. But these agents were too thorough to allow her that much contact with the outside world.

So, now she was formulating a plan involving the only window in the room. Unfortunately, it wasn't an operating window. It was a single pane of glass, fixed in place with wooden trim. And then, of course, there was the matter of a three-story drop, down to the parking lot below. This plan was fizzling fast as she gazed longingly out the window, shading her eyes from the glare of the bright morning sun.

Ginger suddenly caught her breath as she spotted Cinnamon's red Jeep pull into a parking space directly below her window.

"Oh my God!" she exclaimed. "I've got to get her attention." But how? What could she use? It wouldn't do any good to scream. Cinnamon couldn't hear her screams through the glass, but the agents certainly would.

Frantically, she scanned the room and spotted a hand mirror on the dresser. She grabbed it and raced back to the window, holding it up to reflect the sunlight. She twisted and turned the shiny object, trying desperately to direct the beam of light down at Cinnamon.

Finally, she managed to focus the beam on Cinnamon's face. Cinnamon squinted at the bright light, holding up her hand to shield her eyes, but kept walking toward the hotel.

"No!" cried Ginger. "Stop!" Once again, she flashed the beam across Cinnamon's face; and this time, she stopped and looked up. "Yes!" said Ginger, practically out of breath from excitement and desperation. She aimed the mirror down at Cinnamon's feet, then at her chest, letting it rest there a few seconds.

Cinnamon stared at the spot of light on her chest. "What the hell?" She scanned the hotel façade, trying to locate the reflection of light; then looked back down at the spot. The beam moved down onto the sidewalk and back up to her chest.

Okay, she thought, now what. I'm either in someone's line of sight, hopefully not a gun sight, or someone is trying to signal me. The spot of light moved down to the sidewalk and back up, down and back up several times.

Cinnamon looked up at the hotel, but still didn't see anyone. She stared again at the spot on her chest. Once again, it moved down and up, down and up—four times. "Four times," said Cinnamon. She raised four fingers in the air in answer, and the spotlight moved around in a circle on her chest. Four, thought Cinnamon. She knew there wasn't a room number four in the hotel. Fourth floor, perhaps?

She looked up at the narrow windows tucked underneath the roofline and saw a light reflecting in the farthest room on the right. Who would be up there trying to signal to her?

"Oh, my God!" she cried. "Could it be Mother?"

M-O-M she signaled in sign language—the language that Ginger had painstakingly taught all her daughters, so they could communicate with their deaf grandmother. The beam of light danced wildly on her chest.

Cinnamon covered her mouth in astonishment as she fought back tears. Her mother was alive! And she was in this hotel. But, why would the kidnapper keep her here? The fourth floor of the hotel was the owner's residence. She knew Clinton Tate didn't live there, but he owned it. Could he have something to do with the kidnapping or had he simply leased the space to someone else? If that was the case, this kidnapper must be well-funded.

She rushed inside the hotel to find Pepper. They had to rescue their mother. They had to get her out! Frantically, she scanned the lobby looking for Pepper. The two sisters spotted each other at the same time; each anxious to share their recent discoveries.

"There's something important going on up on the fourth floor," said Pepper.

"It's Mother," cried Cinnamon, trying to keep her voice low.

Pepper opened her mouth to scream for joy, but Cinnamon clamped a hand over her mouth to silence her. The ecstatic sisters moved to a deserted corner of the lobby.

"Quiet," said Cinnamon. "I don't want to attract any attention."

"Are you telling me Mother is here?" asked Pepper.

"Yes," whispered Cinnamon. "She signaled to me with a mirror from the fourth floor when I was walking in just now."

"The fourth floor," repeated Pepper. "I just saw a man in a dark suit, wearing a communication device in his ear, go up to the fourth floor."

"A suit?" asked Cinnamon. "And he's keeping her in a five-star hotel? This is the most bizarre case of kidnapping I've ever heard of."

"I thought he was a body guard for a V.I.P.," said Pepper. "Who else would have such high-tech communication equipment?"

"I have no idea," admitted Cinnamon. "These days, everybody's wired—or wireless. But I intend to find out who's keeping Mother on the fourth floor."

"We can't get to the fourth floor without a key for the elevator."

"Damn," said Cinnamon. "I forgot about that. Where can we get a key?"

"I'm sure the front desk has one, but I doubt they'd hand it over to us. Why don't we call Jason? He could get the key."

"No," said Cinnamon. "No police. If they go up there with guns drawn, Mother could wind up in the middle of a gun battle."

Pepper's eyes widen with fear. "What are you planning to do? The kidnapper might shoot us, too!"

"I just want to see who's up there. We can hide on the elevator and take a quick look."

Cinnamon was getting that look in her eye again, and Pepper braced herself for whatever was coming next. "What about the key?"

"Gordon has a key. The kitchen staff uses it to deliver meals to that floor."

"You can't tell him why we need it," argued Pepper.

"You're right. I'll have to steal it."

Pepper gasped. She and Curry weren't quite as bold as Sage and Cinnamon, but what they lacked in spunk, they made up for in spirit.

"I'll need a..."

"I know," said Pepper, reluctantly, "a diversion."

Cinnamon smiled. "Good girl!"

They sneaked down the side hallway leading to the back entrance to the kitchen and peeked in through the small glass window in the swinging door. The kitchen staff was bustling about, preparing for the onslaught of the lunchtime diners.

There was a small desk area just to the left of the door where Gordon handled the restaurant paperwork. The bulletin board above the desk was cluttered with dozens of memos, food orders, and banquet details; and hanging from the bottom right corner, was the elevator key—very conveniently labeled "Fourth Floor."

"I don't think I'll need that diversion after all," said Cinnamon. "If I stay down below the level of the counter, no one can see me."

Pepper held her breath as Cinnamon ducked down and slipped through the swinging door. She was back in a flash, holding the elusive key. "Let's go."

Pepper, in her high-heeled Ferragamo's, clattered along at break-neck speed behind Cinnamon's long strides. They sidled up to the elevator, slipped inside and inserted the key. For better or worse, they were on their way to the top.

"Your phone," said Pepper. "Turn it off. You don't want it to ring while you're nosing around."

"Thanks for reminding me."

Cinnamon winced as the elevator bell dinged loudly when they reached the top floor. "I hope that didn't announce our arrival to everyone up here."

They each pressed themselves flat against the front corners of the elevator as the doors slid open. Pepper pressed the "door open" button, as they peeked out into the hallway. The coast was clear.

"You wait here and hold the elevator," whispered Cinnamon. "I'll take a look."

Pepper nodded. She was so scared her knees were shaking. How much more adrenaline could her body take in one day?

Cinnamon crept down the short, carpeted hallway, her heart pounding loudly in her ears. There were four rooms opening out onto this end of the hallway, but only one door was closed. That would be my pick, thought Cinnamon, as she placed her ear against the door and listened carefully. She couldn't hear any sounds in the room, so she knocked lightly.

"Come in," said Ginger.

Cinnamon's heart began to race, as she fumbled with the key that was in the lock to open the door slightly and then peeked inside.

"Cinnamon," cried Ginger, rushing over to hug her daughter.

"Mother, are you all right? We've been so worried about you."

"I'm fine," replied Ginger, "but they wouldn't let me call you."

"Who?" asked Cinnamon. "Who kidnapped you?"

Ginger heard a man's voice out in the hallway.

"Shh!" she said, pushing Cinnamon back behind the door.

Peter stepped inside the room, with a questioning glance at Ginger. "I thought I heard voices in here," he said. "Who opened this door?"

He took a step toward Ginger, as Cinnamon grabbed a large lamp off the dresser and held it over her head. This kidnapper was about to have his lights knocked out.

"No!" screamed Ginger. "He's an F.B.I. agent."

Peter spun around, coming nose-to-nose with the five-foot, ten-inch Cinnamon. She found herself staring into the dreamiest blue eyes she had seen in...well, hell—ever! An F.B.I. agent, she thought, glancing down at his broad shoulders and trim waist, and she knew, if she could see the other side, this package would include a tight butt, too. Her body tingled in places she hadn't felt in a long time. She really needed to get a social life.

"Do you want to put down that lamp or am I going to have to shoot you?" he said in a sexy voice, followed by more tingling on her part.

"I'm sorry, Peter," said Ginger. "This is Cinnamon, my daughter."

"Cinnamon?" he asked, letting his eyes wander up and down the attractive young woman's well-toned body, with those sparkling hazel eyes and bad-ass red hair. "Now let me get this straight," he said. "You're Ginger, your husband is Mace, and your daughter is Cinnamon. Do I detect a pattern here?"

"Peter," said Agent Johnson, dragging a sullen Pepper behind him. "Look what I found skulking in the elevator. She says she's..."

"Mother!" cried Pepper.

"Pepper!" cried Ginger.

"Yep, that's what she said," replied Agent Johnson.

Peter chuckled. "I love it. A whole set of spices."

Cinnamon scowled at him.

"Well, not quite the whole set," said Ginger, smiling at her two daughters.

"You mean there are more?" he asked.

"Yes," my oldest daughter is Sage and Curry is Pepper's twin."

Peter shook his head in amazement; then his gaze landed on Agent Johnson.

"How the hell did these two manage to get past you, Johnson?"

"I had to take a l-l-l...break," Ted groused. "And Harriet was gone."

Peter shot a furtive glance at Cinnamon. "How did you get a key to the elevator?"

She stared right back. "I stole it from the hotel chef."

Peter paused—apparently this feisty spirit was a family trait. "And how did you know your mother was here?"

"She signaled to me."

Peter looked at Ginger in amazement. "I used a mirror," she explained, proudly.

"You took a big risk coming up here," he said to Cinnamon, admiring her spunk. "Real kidnappers would have shot you on sight."

"My mother wouldn't have put me in that kind of danger," retorted Cinnamon. "But speaking of kidnappers—when did the F.B.I. get in to the kidnapping business?"

"We took Ginger into protective custody," countered Peter. "Maybelle Jamison was murdered by an arms dealer in this area because she discovered his identity and confronted him. He was going to kill Ginger next, in case Maybelle leaked any information to her."

Pepper and Cinnamon gasped as they looked at their mother.

"Did she tell you anything?" asked Cinnamon

"I think she said 'Applewhite'," replied Ginger.

Cinnamon looked at Peter, "Who is Applewhite?"

"We don't know yet," he replied. "It's just a code name for the arms dealer, but we believe he's a hotel employee."

"So what do we do now?" asked Cinnamon.

Peter looked at her, flabbergasted. "You're not going to do anything. You and Pepper are now in protective custody along with your mother. We can't compromise our surveillance."

"There's not a chance in hell you can keep us hidden here," exclaimed Cinnamon. "My sisters know we came here, and our cars are parked out front. Don't you think they're going to come looking for us? Sage will turn this hotel inside out. You can forget about your surveillance if she finds out you've kidnapped us."

Peter glanced at Ginger for guidance. "Sage is a lawyer," she explained.

He rubbed the back of his neck to ease the mounting tension. How did this operation get so screwed up in such a short period of time?

"Peter," said Agent Harriet Blair. "It seems that we have a situation over at Congressman Jamison's office. There's a Sheriff Winters on the line who needs to talk to you."

"Jason?" asked Cinnamon.

"He's not part of your family, too, is he?" asked the exasperated Peter.

"No," replied Ginger. "He's just a family friend. Although, Mace and I keep hoping that he and Sage can work out their differences. They really do belong together."

Peter stared in disbelief. Had he been dropped into the "Twilight Zone"? "Is there anybody in this town you don't know?" he asked, still rubbing the back of his neck, as the tension continued to mount.

"It's a small town," replied Cinnamon, smiling at him and getting that tingly feeling all over again.

"I'll be back," he said, heading for the door. Then he turned and shook his finger at Cinnamon, "Don't...You just...Oh, hell," he shrugged. "Johnson, get that damned elevator key!"

Chapter Nine

Congressman Henry Jamison jammed his cell phone down into his suit coat pocket and ran toward the men's room at Dulles Airport outside Washington, D.C. He barely made it in time to throw up into the toilet; thankfully missing his expensive, highly polished Italian leather shoes. He was a total wreck—no, actually he was a dead man.

His daughter, Cynthia, had just called to tell him a bomb exploded in his Clearwater office, leaving two of his employees dead and a third hospitalized in critical condition. She also informed him that a couple of Morgan County Sheriff's Deputies would be waiting for him when his plane arrived at Bush Intercontinental Airport in Houston. The situation for the Congressman had gone from bad to worse.

Ever since Maybelle called him Wednesday night about the journal she found—his private journal—the one describing every minute detail of his transactions with Applewhite for the past two years, he had been scared out of his mind. He hadn't slept or been able to keep any food in his stomach for three days.

That damned Maybelle had gotten herself killed because she couldn't keep her mouth shut. And now, they were going to kill him, too, because the Sheriff (and God knows who else) was investigating her murder. If they found that journal, Henry Jamison was screwed. The Feds would throw him in jail for the rest of his life—which really didn't matter because Applewhite would make sure he didn't have any time left in his life. He was screwed either way.

Henry realized now that keeping that journal was a stupid mistake. But he was so caught up in the excitement and intrigue of secret operations and foreign arms deals, he couldn't resist recording his part in this espionage scenario; planning to write a best-selling novel to cash in on the experience from another angle. In retrospect, he realized that his own ego was about to cost him his life.

He had to sneak back into Clearwater, find that damned journal, grab his passport and get out of the country. Changing his identity and living in some third-world country with no extradition policy was the only option he had left.

After all those years he wasted sucking up to those pompous assholes on Capitol Hill, he finally found a way to make it all pay off. It was such a sweet deal. All he had to do was arrange for Applewhite's cohorts to get onto several military bases, where they loaded up and shipped out millions of dollars worth of arms—right under the U.S. Government's nose. And he was paid five million dollars for every visit, deposited anonymously in an off-shore bank account, safe from the eyes of Uncle Sam. He had fifteen million dollars in that account now, but there would have been more if Maybelle hadn't ruined the whole deal.

He deserved every penny of it, too. He spent fifteen years in public service, only to be tossed out like garbage. He paid his dues, played along with the "good old boy" political network, and even managed to grab a few dollars from the pork barrel for his constituents. But they didn't show him one ounce of gratitude—not one iota of respect.

It would serve the American people right if those terrorists took over this country. Hell, half of the eligible voters don't even bother to vote in most elections. Maybe if they had to fight to get their freedom back, they might actually appreciate it. They're all just a bunch of whining parasites, expecting the government to give them a hand-out. He was sick of it.

Of course, his deal with Applewhite was about to come to a screeching halt anyway, since the party decided he was expendable. They needed Henry's seat in the House to groom a new hot-shot party favorite for higher office, so they politely told him to take a hike. Without his political connections, he couldn't arrange for any more military base pillaging. Applewhite's arms dealing business would be in limbo until he could recruit another accomplice.

Henry had big plans for that money, too. He pledged twenty million toward a real estate development deal in Costa Rica with Clinton Tate, but that deal was a bust now. He'd have to take the money he had left and buy a new identity in a foreign country. But first, he had to find that journal—without getting caught.

If those deputies were waiting for him at Bush Airport, he'd need to change his plans. He flushed the toilet and couldn't help but compare it to his own life at the moment, because that's exactly where it was. After splashing cold water on his face in a futile attempt to quell his nausea, he glanced at his reflection in the mirror. His once fashionably tanned face was a sickly shade of pale green and dark circles underscored his lifeless blue eyes.

He turned away in disgust. For Henry, his outward appearance was all that mattered—expensive hand-tailored suits, perfectly trimmed and dyed hair, and a lean and well-toned body. He was a proud and vain man, and he desperately needed to reclaim his "power image".

Henry hurried over to the airline ticket counter to change his flight reservations.

"I'll need a flight into Hobby Airport instead," he told the ticket agent.

"There aren't any direct flights from Dulles into Hobby," she explained.

"No problem," he replied. "I don't mind a longer flight." As a matter of fact, arriving after dark would be even better. He planned to rent a car at the airport, sneak into Clearwater, pick up his passport and hopefully the journal, and then head back to the airport and book the next flight out of the country; to anywhere.

Henry was starting to feel better already. He might just stop at a café and have a bite to eat before boarding the plane. And he knew exactly what he wanted, so he headed for his favorite airport restaurant, Louie's Bar and Grill. They made the best crab cakes on the planet. His mouth began to water as he thought about those golden fried, spicy crab cakes. And he planned to wash them down with his favorite cocktail—a double Manhattan. Things were definitely looking up.

What he failed to notice, however, was the virtual parade of characters following him around the airport. There was the tall young man wearing a dark business suit and talking into a wireless communication device in his ear—definitely F.B.I. Then there was the Chief of Airport Security, who had been put on alert by the

Morgan County Sheriff's Office. And last was a middle-age, slightly balding, average looking citizen, reading a local newspaper—an Applewhite informant.

All of them managed to be within ear-shot when the Congressman made his new flight reservations, but Henry was blissfully unaware of their presence. He safely boarded his plane and actually managed to take a short nap during his flight, feeling quite confident that he had foiled the Sheriff's plan to intercept him at Bush Airport.

* * * * * * * * * *

Jason returned from the bomb scene in Old Towne to find a flurry of activity at the office. The Chief of Security at Dulles Airport had put in a call to Sheriff Jason Winters as soon as he heard Congressman Jamison change his flight reservations from Bush Airport to Hobby. Jason returned his call immediately.

"It looks like he's on the run," said the Chief. "He's either trying to avoid interrogation by the police or he's running scared from someone else. Do you want me to take him into custody?"

"No," replied Jason. "We'll be there to pick him up at Hobby. I'm calling the F.B.I. to see what their take is on this situation. It's gone beyond my limited resources, and I plan to let them take over from here. Thanks for your help, Chief."

Jason hung up the phone and then listened to an excited Deputy Sam Davis's account of the break-in at Mace McCormick's house and the evidence left behind. He was one hundred percent sure now that he needed some backup with this case, so he placed a call to the F.B.I. Field Office in Houston. Sage was right, this was something big, evil and powerful, and he needed help fighting it.

It was obvious to Jason that this same group had murdered Maybelle, kidnapped Ginger, followed Sage, and bombed the Congressman's office. He desperately hoped they could find a match for the finger prints on the gun left behind at the McCormick house. It was the only evidence they had.

Henry Jamison was somehow involved in this scenario, but he was too scared to talk to the police about it. And Jason feared there wasn't much hope of getting Ginger back alive. But why was this group on the rampage in Clearwater? Was it organized crime or terrorists? What did they want?

The minute the F.B.I. Field Office agent heard Sheriff Winters say "Clearwater," he was transferred immediately to Special Agent Peter Dalton, currently on assignment in the area.

"This is Special Agent Dalton," said Peter, when Harriet handed him the phone.

"Agent Dalton, this is Sheriff Jason Winters in Clearwater. I understand that you are on a special assignment here."

"That's correct," replied Peter. "How can I help you, Sheriff?"

Jason explained the crime spree currently plaguing the small town, including Maybelle's murder, Ginger's kidnapping, Sage's car chase, the office bombing, the disappearance of Cinnamon and Pepper, the break-in at the McCormick's house and his suspicions about Henry Jamison.

"I'm convinced that all these crimes were committed by the same group of people, but I don't have a clue who or why," said the disheartened Sheriff. "Can you shed any light on this situation?"

"Yes," confirmed Peter. "You're right. Most of those crimes were committed by the same group. For the past two years, we've been tracking an arms dealer in this area who sells weapons to terrorists. All we know about him is his code name, 'Applewhite,' and that he operates out of The Grand Hotel. We believe he's a hotel employee. Maybelle discovered his identity and he killed her. Unfortunately, Ginger McCormick was accidentally thrown into the mix, so we took her into protective custody to keep Applewhite from killing her, too. It seems that Maybelle tried to tell Ginger about the dealer before she died."

"So Ginger is with you now and she's safe?" asked Jason.

"Yes, she's fine. We're holding her here on the fourth floor of The Grand Hotel, which is also the base for our surveillance operation."

"Thank God. But what about Cinnamon and Pepper?"

"The two amateur sleuths?" asked Peter. "They're here, too. They actually managed to infiltrate our safe house."

"Yeah, that sounds about right," chuckled Jason. "So you have them all at The Grand Hotel?" he laughed again, first from sheer relief at hearing they were all safe, then at the thought of Special Agent Dalton trying to keep them all corralled.

"I take it you know this group of spice women fairly well."

"Yes. They can be a handful."

"That's an understatement," confessed Peter. "I've been thinking about adding them to the team. They are quite resourceful and persistent."

"And don't forget feisty," added Jason. "So what's the plan now? Can I tell Ginger's family that she's safe?"

"You can tell them, but I can't release her, Sheriff. We still don't know who Applewhite is, and he knows where we're holding her. He's already tried once to kill her, right here in the hotel."

Jason sobered with that thought. "What can I do? Should we try to move her to another location? The man who attacked Mace said his group already assumed that you had moved her."

"I don't see how we could sneak her out of the hotel," replied Peter, "even though this group probably expects us to do just that. I feel it's best to sit tight and increase our security rather than set up a new operation in another location.

"We believe Applewhite operates out of this hotel; it's why we set up our surveillance team here. But we haven't figured out yet who he is. I would appreciate it if you'd let us know as soon as your lab completes the search on the finger prints you found on the gun. Maybe it will lead to more names."

"I hope so, too," replied Jason. "The only other information I found out—well actually Curry found out—is that Maybelle said she was planning to clean house when she took over the hotel, and get rid of the 'riff-raff'. The two employees we know she was talking about are Glen Durst, the hotel manager, who is now in jail, and Gordon Ellis, the head chef.

"I just ran a background check on Ellis," Jason continued, "and all the information I received checks out. There was nothing in his record to indicate that he is involved in any type of criminal activity, and he has an alibi for Maybelle's murder."

"Yes, we checked him out, too," said Peter. "He was born in Indiana, graduated from Berkley University, trained at the Cordon Bleu in Paris, taught at the culinary school in New York, and then wound up here two years ago."

"What about the hotel owner, Clinton Tate? Did you find anything on him?" asked Jason.

"We were suspicious when we found out he was selling all his developments in Clearwater and planning to move to Costa Rica. But, so far we've come up empty handed as far as arms connections."

"Obviously, Henry Jamison is involved in this operation somehow or he wouldn't be trying to avoid us, unless he feels threatened because Maybelle told him about Applewhite, too," said Jason. "But if that was the case, I think he'd be running to the F.B.I. for protection."

"I agree, but unless he's willing to talk to us, we'll have to find hard evidence to connect him to Applewhite. We've had over fifty million dollars worth of weapons stolen from several military bases over the past couple of years. The Congressman has access to those bases, but that doesn't prove he was involved."

"So where do we go from here?" asked Jason.

"Your guess is as good as mine, Sheriff. We're stumped. Maybe we should turn the spice sisters loose on him."

Jason chuckled. "That might not be such a crazy idea. I'll tell Mace, Sage and Curry that the rest of their family is safe. I'm sure we can trust them to keep quiet."

"That's fine," agreed Peter. "From what I've seen of this family so far, it would be a plus to have them on our side."

"Absolutely," replied Jason. "You don't want to find yourself on the opposing side when you're dealing with the spice sisters. They're a formidable team."

Jason paused for a moment. "Would it help to have more manpower posted at the hotel? I can spare a few deputies if you need them."

"I could definitely use some backup," replied Peter.

Jason hung up the phone with mixed emotions. He was elated that Ginger, Pepper and Cinnamon were fine. He also felt somewhat relieved that the F.B.I. was sharing the burden of fighting this sinister force that had invaded Clearwater. But this battle was far from over. They were all still in danger until Applewhite was caught.

At least he had solved one mystery. He jumped in his squad car, and headed for the McCormick house to share the news about Ginger, Cinnamon and Pepper.

A relieved Sage answered the door when she realized the unexpected visitor ringing the doorbell was Jason. She searched his face anxiously for clues about Ginger—was it good news or bad news?

He smiled at her. She grabbed him by the arm and yanked him inside. Mace and Curry rushed to greet him, also hoping for good news.

"Did you find Ginger?" asked Mace. "And Cinnamon and Pepper?"

"Yes," replied Jason. "They're all fine."

"Oh, thank God!" said Sage. "Have a seat. I have a feeling this is going to be a long story."

Jason nodded and settled into one of the family room chairs. Mace and Curry perched on the edge of the sofa, while Sage plopped down onto the floor at Jason's feet.

"Maybelle was killed by an arms dealer operating here in Clearwater, because she discovered his identity," said Jason. "All we know about him is that his code name is 'Applewhite,' and we think he's an employee at The Grand Hotel. Ginger just happened to be in the wrong place at the wrong time and got tangled up in this mess by mistake, but he was planning to kill her, too.

"The F.B.I. has been tracking this dealer for two years, and finally narrowed his location to Clearwater, so they set up their surveillance operation on the fourth floor of the hotel. They realized Ginger was in danger after Maybelle was killed, so they took her into protective custody."

"So the man who broke into the house today was right," said Mace, "the F.B.I. kidnapped Ginger."

"Yes," confirmed Jason. "Deputy Davis told me about the man who attacked you this morning. We're running the prints from the gun now. Hopefully, we'll have a match soon."

"It would have been better if we had caught the guy," complained Mace. "I'm sure he's already reported to Applewhite that Ginger isn't here, and they need to be on the alert for F.B.I. surveillance."

"The F.B.I. agents still have Ginger on the fourth floor of The Grand Hotel, but they beefed up their security after the arms dealer's group tried to get to her. I've also sent extra deputies over there for backup. We're afraid to move her to another location at this point. We think we have a better chance of keeping her safe where she is now."

"What about Cinnamon and Pepper," asked Curry. "How did they wind up on the fourth floor with Mother?"

"Ginger managed to send a signal to Cinnamon when she arrived at the hotel this morning. Cinnamon and Pepper went up to the fourth floor to find her, but Special Agent Peter Dalton, who's heading up the operation, caught them. They are now in protective custody, as well."

"That was crazy," exclaimed Curry. "What were they thinking?"

"We would have done the same thing," countered Sage. "At least they're safe."

"We believe this dealer or one of his associates is responsible for your car chase, Sage, as well as the office bombing," said Jason. "We also think Henry Jamison is involved. He's trying to avoid talking to us at the moment, but I'm sending a couple of deputies to pick him up at the airport at five o'clock. Hopefully, we can get him to tell us the name of the arms dealer. Until we capture him, Ginger, Cinnamon and Pepper will have to remain in protective custody."

"Who are your suspects?" asked Sage.

"Clinton Tate is one, but so far, we haven't found any connections to arms dealers or terrorist groups. Gordon Ellis is the other suspect, but his background checks out, and he has an alibi for the time of Maybelle's murder."

"So, what do we do now?" asked Sage. "Look for more suspects?"

"Agent Dalton is doing more checks on Tate's Costa Rica deals, and I plan to double check Gordon Ellis' alibi. He and Jenny Hall both claim they were in a meeting together at the time of the murder. We'll interrogate Henry Jamison when he arrives."

"What can we do to help?" asked Mace.

"There's really nothing you can do at this point," replied Jason. "Don't tell anyone about the F.B.I.'s involvement or that they have Ginger, Cinnamon and Pepper."

Mace nodded. "Is there any way I can talk to Ginger?"

"Not yet. I'm sending some deputies over to the hotel for extra manpower—she should be safe, Mace. They will all be fine."

Sage had been uncharacteristically quiet while he revealed the latest details of this saga, and that made Jason nervous. "Are you okay?" he asked her, now searching her face for clues the same way she had searched his earlier.

"I'm fine," she replied, with a thin smile. But that smile didn't reach her eyes. Those eyes were scheming and plotting. It looked like this ride might be heading for a few more dips and turns. Like he said before, he planned to hang on tight.

Chapter Ten

After Jason's visit with the McCormick family, he returned to his office. It was only three o'clock. The Congressman's rescheduled flight wouldn't arrive until five, which gave him a couple of hours to confirm Gordon Ellis's alibi. He planned to have another chat with Jenny Hall. She was off work for the weekend, so he dialed her home phone. When the answering machine picked up, he left a message that he needed to talk to her. Jason wanted to question Gordon, too, but he preferred to hear Jenny's version first.

He drummed his fingers on his graffiti-covered desk pad. He couldn't just sit around and wait, so he tucked Jenny's address into his shirt pocket and headed out for a drive. She lived in one of the new condo complexes a few blocks off the bay. Even if she wasn't home, he figured the drive would get him away from the chaotic office for a while, so he could think.

During all the years he worked as a detective in Houston, he never encountered a case like this one. He thought moving to a small county would be less stressful, and it had been, until this crime spree began. But then, he hadn't dealt with an organized group of arms dealers before either. The only gang activities he had ever encountered were the low-level punks who formed their own territorial gangs around Houston.

They had no money or power, and certainly no brains. Their crimes were limited to drug sales, occasional knife fights and burglary—nothing on the scale of this arms dealer, Applewhite. He was obviously well funded and had access to a huge network of resources, mostly illegal.

Jason turned his vehicle into Jenny's complex and cruised by row after row of two-story, beige stucco units until he spotted her address. Each unit had an enclosed front courtyard with a wooden gate and an attached garage at the back, accessed by an alley. He parked in front of her unit and walked up to the gate.

There was a lively game of volleyball in progress in the park across the street, and the rowdy group of young men laughed and shouted as they slapped the ball back and forth over the net. Several families were enjoying the mild weather with a Saturday picnic in the park. He could smell the smoke from their barbecue grills. Life goes on, he thought, even in the midst of chaos.

He stepped through the gate and crossed the tiny, perfectly landscaped courtyard, but when he reached out to ring the doorbell, he noticed the front door was ajar. He opened the door slightly and called out to Jenny. "Miss Hall, are you here? It's Sheriff Winters."

He heard no response, so he opened the door wider and peered into the entry way. Books and clothing were strewn carelessly on the floor. Sensing that something was wrong, he entered the unit and stopped short at the sight of mass destruction. Broken glass, food containers, clothing and photographs littered the floor. The upholstered furniture was slashed, with stuffing hanging out in huge wads. Framed pictures were torn off the walls and smashed, and the curtains hung in shreds.

"What the hell happened? Miss Hall, are you in here?" he shouted.

Jason ran up the stairs into the only bedroom where the destruction continued. Jenny Hall was nowhere in sight. A broken photo frame lay on the bedside table, but the photograph was gone. He checked the bathroom and closets, but didn't find her. There was no way to gauge whether or not any of her personal possessions were missing, because everything was scattered all over the floor and countertops. But he didn't see any evidence of bloodshed, which was a good sign.

Finally, he checked the garage. It was empty. Did an intruder take Jenny or did she leave on her own before the destruction occurred? Questions were coming at him a mile-a-minute. He punched on his radio and called for a crime scene unit, then told dispatch to issue an APB on Jenny's vehicle.

He had been blindsided by this turn of events. Was Jenny Hall caught in this arms dealer's net, too? She was a hotel employee; maybe she found out the same information Maybelle did, and Maybelle was murdered because of it. When would this nightmare end? He was doing everything he could to stop it, but he seemed to be losing ground. Thank God he had Peter Dalton's support to back him up, because he was about ready to throw in the towel. He had no idea where this group would strike next, and he felt powerless to stop them.

It was too depressing to stay in the violated condo unit while he waited for the deputies to arrive, so he stepped out into the peaceful courtyard. He breathed in the cool crisp air, trying to get his emotions under control, listening to the sounds of laughter from the volleyball court. As an investigator, it was important for him to remain emotionally detached from the crime. He couldn't let his emotions cloud his judgment, which could lead to false and sometimes costly assumptions. The stakes in this investigation were too high. He couldn't afford to make such foolish mistakes.

After the crime scene unit began processing the evidence, Jason hit the road again. This time he headed for The Grand Hotel to get Gordon Ellis's take on Jenny Hall's disappearance. On the way there, he put in a call to Agent Dalton. "Jenny Hall has disappeared," he said, "and her condo was torn to shreds. I'm on my way to talk to Gordon Ellis now. I was trying to confirm his alibi with Jenny, but it looks like that's not going to be possible."

"Do you think she could be another Applewhite victim?" asked Peter.

"I have no idea," admitted Jason. "Ginger works with Jenny as a wedding planner. Could you find out what she knows about Jenny—especially what her relationship was with Gordon?"

"Will do," replied Peter. "When you're finished questioning Gordon, come up to the fourth floor and we'll compare notes."

"I'll be there."

*　*　*　*　*　*　*　*　*　*

Jason crossed the hotel lobby and hurried down the side hallway, which led to the back entrance to the kitchen. He peered through the window in the swinging door at the frazzled kitchen staff, scurrying about in preparation for the dinner rush. Gordon Ellis was perched on a stool at his desk, laboring over a lengthy food order.

Jason stepped into the noisy, overheated, but deliciously aromatic space. "I need to ask you a few questions, Gordon, if you have a minute."

Gordon glanced over at the frantic kitchen crew, then back at Jason. "Sure. How can I help you, Sheriff?"

"I just came from Jenny Hall's condo. It's been ransacked, and she appears to be missing."

Gordon's eyebrows shot up in surprise. "I'm sorry to hear that. Do you think it was burglary?"

"Not really," Jason frowned, flashing back on the senseless destruction. "How well do you know Miss Hall?"

"We've worked together planning events since I became head chef here two years ago. But all I know about her personally is that she's single and lives alone."

"You've had no contact with her socially, outside of work?"

"None," replied Gordon. "She isn't exactly my type, Sheriff."

Jason paused, expectantly.

"She's a nice person," continued Gordon, "and very attractive; but just a tad 'ditzy'. Kind of like a Barbie doll on saccharine."

Jason glared at him, but Gordon just shrugged.

"Did she mention anything to you about leaving town? Or that she might have been in some kind of trouble?"

"No, Sheriff. The last time I talked to her was Friday morning during our meeting in the Yellow Rose Ballroom at ten o'clock. Like I told you yesterday, we were discussing a buffet layout when we heard all the commotion in the lobby. We ran to the staircase and saw Maybelle and Ginger at the bottom of the stairs. I didn't see Jenny for the rest of the day, and she wasn't scheduled to work this weekend."

"Is there anyone else at the hotel who knows more about her personal life?"

"Well, Glen Durst might. The two of them seemed to be rather cozy, if you get my drift."

Jason narrowed his eyes, deep in thought. He hadn't considered the possibility that Jenny's disappearance could be connected to Glen. If Maybelle knew about his embezzled millions, maybe Jenny did, too. But that didn't explain the destruction at her condo, unless it was a set-up to make them believe she had been kidnapped—like Ginger. In any case, he wasn't making much headway in this interrogation, so he decided to move on.

"Okay, Gordon. Thanks for your time."

Jason jotted a few notes in his notebook and headed for the elevator, making a quick call to Peter. A few minutes later, the elevator doors opened, and he was greeted with a handshake by a tall, dark-haired man in his mid-thirties.

"Sheriff, I'm Special Agent Peter Dalton."

"Jason Winters," he replied, stepping into the elevator.

"How'd the interview go?" asked Peter.

"Didn't take me where I thought it would, but I've either been thrown off the trail by a good liar, or I might have a new lead."

When they reached the fourth floor, Peter led Jason into a small sitting area to confer before meeting with Ginger. "Do you think Jenny Hall's disappearance is related to our arms dealer?"

"At first I thought it might be, but Gordon says she was in a relationship with Glen Durst."

"Ah," mused Peter. "The missing five million dollars."

"Yeah. I've got an APB out on her vehicle. We'll see what turns up. Unfortunately, with Jenny gone, I can't challenge Gordon's alibi."

"We just found out Clinton Tate's business partner for the Costa Rica project is Henry Jamison," said Peter. "Clinton told us they each pledged twenty million for the development."

"Whew," whistled Jason. "I know the Congressman is rich, but he's been out of the development business for a long time. That's a serious chunk of change. Have you checked his financial records?"

"We did. If he's got it, it's hidden somewhere out of the country."

"Hidden from the I.R.S. you mean. No wonder he's running scared. Do you think he's involved with the military base thefts?"

"Things are looking pretty bad for Henry Jamison right now. You have two deputies meeting him at Hobby?"

"Yeah, at five o'clock. We're going to have a lot to talk about with the Congressman."

Peter nodded. "Do you still want to talk to Ginger?"

Jason smiled, "Sure." As they left the sitting room, Jason took a deep breath. "What's that wonderful aroma? Is someone cooking up here?"

"That would be our newly acquired resident chef, Cinnamon," replied Peter. "I believe, right now, she's preparing her famous 'Cinnamon Apple Pork Tenderloin'. This suite has a kitchen, and apparently she goes into non-stop cooking mode when she's bored or stressed. And she's both at the moment."

Jason laughed. "Lucky for you. Have you tasted her cooking?"

"Not yet. She won't let me near the place, but she's got everyone on this floor drooling. If it keeps her off my case and everyone fed, more power to her."

Peter retrieved a key from his pocket and unlocked Ginger's door. "Just an extra precaution," he explained when he noticed Jason's puzzled look. "They've gotten in before. I'm not going to let it happen again."

He gave a light knock on the door before opening it, and then let Jason go in ahead of him.

"Jason," cried Ginger, running to give him a hug. "It's so good to see you. Did you tell Mace I'm okay?"

"Yes, I told Mace, Sage and Curry. They know you're here with Cinnamon and Pepper."

"Thank you. I'll be so glad when this nightmare is over and I can go home. Not that you haven't been nice, Peter," she added apologetically. "But...well...you know what I mean."

Peter nodded, stifling a smile at the motherly Ginger. It was part of her nature to be a caregiver. Now that her daughters were grown, she transferred her "need to mother" onto her brides, herding them around like baby ducklings; and they loved it. Ginger's wedding planning expertise was in high demand.

"I need to ask you a few questions about Jenny Hall," said Jason.

"Oh, yes. Peter told me that her condo was torn apart and she was missing," exclaimed Ginger. "Do you think she was kidnapped by Applewhite?"

"I don't think so. Her car was gone, too, which leads me to believe she left on her own. But we still don't know why her condo was ransacked. Gordon says she was in a relationship with Glen Durst. Do you know anything about her personal life?"

"Not really. I just worked with her in planning events for my brides. Jenny was...well," Ginger paused, trying to be as tactful as she could, "she was...really sweet."

Jason grimaced, remembering Gordon's saccharine comment.

"But she was a bit wishy-washy when it came to making decisions," added Ginger, "which can cause problems when coordinating large events."

"So, she wasn't very good at her job?" asked Jason. "Who hired her?"

"I think Glen did. They were from the same town in Illinois."

Jason and Peter glanced at each other, as a few puzzle pieces clicked into place.

"Oh, dear," said Ginger. "Do you think Jenny had something to do with stealing that money in Chicago?"

"It's beginning to look that way," replied Jason. "Thanks, Ginger. You've been a big help."

The two lawmen returned to the elevator. "Do you want to be present when I question Henry Jamison?" asked Jason.

"No. Just let me know what he says. I'm not really expecting much; he'll probably clam up and call a lawyer. Our only hope is to find some hard evidence linking him to Applewhite."

Jason nodded in agreement. Peter returned to his office, while Jason waited for the elevator. Sage was right about those loopholes. They seemed to be getting bigger instead of smaller. Before the elevator arrived, his cell phone rang. It was the Sheriff in Trenton County, a few hundred miles south of Clearwater.

"We picked up your missing female," he said. "She was about to cross the border into Mexico. Do you have any warrants for her arrest?"

"Not yet," replied Jason. "But you might want to get her finger prints and run a background check on her. I've got a sneaking suspicion she was involved in an embezzlement scheme in Chicago about five years ago. We just arrested David Groves, a.k.a. Glen Durst for the same crime. We think she might be his accomplice."

"If that's the case," replied the Trenton County Sheriff, "I don't think this little blonde Barbie doll was the brains of the outfit."

Jason chuckled. "Apparently that's the prevailing consensus. Let me know what you turn up."

"Will do."

Jason sighed with relief, thankful that he didn't need to add Jenny Hall to the list of Applewhite's victims. He pressed the elevator button, anxious to get back to his office before his detectives delivered Henry Jamison. Jason was convinced that Henry held the key to solving this mystery, but how could they force him to talk?

Chapter Eleven

Pepper McCormick lay on the chaise in the beautifully appointed bedroom Agent Peter Dalton had assigned to her after being captured that morning during Cinnamon's impromptu rescue mission. She was ecstatic to learn that her mother was safe and not in the hands of Maybelle's killer, but appalled to discover that she and Cinnamon would be held captive, as well.

She realized that this situation was in her mother's best interest. Applewhite's operatives had already tried to kill Ginger once, and she certainly didn't want them to get another chance, but she was bored out of her skull. The minute Cinnamon discovered the gourmet kitchen located conveniently on their floor, she was lost in her world of cooking. She was in her element, which enabled her to put this terrorist threat on a back burner, so to speak. But Pepper had no release from her boredom and stress.

She was an innovative and talented young fashion designer. In the clothing business she shared with Curry, Pepper usually sketched the new designs and Curry converted her sketches into patterns. Then their seamstresses used the patterns to produce the clothing they sold to their wealthy clientele.

Her design vision was not unlike that of an interior designer, who looks at a room and automatically envisions the finished design—complete with color scheme, furniture styles, lighting and layout. Whenever Pepper saw a piece of fabric, she knew instantly how it should be cut, draped and fitted on a human form in order to show it off to its best advantage. She could do the same thing when looking at the human form, no matter what shape or size, and envision the most flattering design for that particular figure.

She worked with many of Ginger's brides, who were faced with the daunting task of finding flattering bridesmaid's dresses for a wide variety of female shapes. A bride has enough details to worry about without facing the wrath of her friends and family members over her choice of wedding attire. Pepper always managed to find the perfect solution to make each bridesmaid feel attractive and special.

But today, her creative mind felt like a ticking time bomb and her fingers were itching for the feel of a sketching pencil. She jumped up from the chaise and ran over to the small writing desk, searching the drawers for paper and any kind of writing utensil, but found all the drawers empty. This is not going to work at all, she thought, flopping back down onto the velvet chaise. I'm going to go insane in this place if I can't even sketch.

She glanced around the beautifully decorated room, trying to get an inkling of inspiration from the fabrics. The draperies were heavy, olive green velvet. The fabric reminded her of Scarlett O'Hara's drapery dress in *Gone with the Wind*. Yuck—definitely not inspiring. The comforter on the bed was antique white silk, stitched into a puffy down quilt. A wedding gown for an outdoor ceremony at the North Pole, perhaps? She just wasn't feeling it.

Maybe the closet would yield something more exciting, she thought, throwing open the heavy double doors. Extra blankets, pillows, and sheets—what did she expect; it was a hotel. But she did discover four large cardboard shipping boxes stacked against the left wall.

To snoop or not to snoop, she wondered, with a guilty glance around the room. Why not? She had nothing better to do. Maybe this activity would keep her occupied for a while, not to mention preventing her from going stir-crazy.

She lifted the top box off the stack and set it down on the floor of the closet. It was so light it felt empty. The flaps weren't even taped closed—a definite sign that snoopers were welcome. She opened the flaps and peeked inside. It was filled to the top with white Styrofoam "peanuts".

Disappointed so far, she stuck her hand down into the fluffy bits and stirred them around in search of treasure. Her hand bumped against the sharp corner of an envelope. She gasped with surprise and pulled out a medium-size tan envelope; spilling the peanuts all over the floor.

"Damn, what a mess," she said, scooping up the bits of foam and trying to drop them back into the box. But the static cling caused them to stick to her fingers. "Damn," she said again, impatiently shaking her hands, trying to force the little monsters to let go. Finally, she gave up and wiped her hands on her skirt, which, of course, transferred the obnoxious debris to her clothing. "To hell with it," she cried, finally admitting defeat in the battle of the foam. She gladly abandoned her cleaning chore, anxious to explore the contents of the envelope.

Inside, she found a large skeleton key. "How bizarre," she said. "One key packed in a huge box full of peanuts." She laid the key aside and checked the contents of the remaining three boxes. No more keys—just peanuts. "Well, that was a bust," she said, sitting on the closet floor in the middle of a pile of white Styrofoam bits.

But her afternoon adventure wasn't over yet. She noticed a small door in the wall where the boxes had been stacked. It was about two feet wide and four feet tall, with a beautiful crystal door knob and a keyhole underneath. Pepper smiled, "Well, now. Let's just see if the key fits." She was beginning to feel like "Alice in Wonderland".

The key slipped easily into the hole and turned effortlessly. The lock clicked open and Pepper peered through the open door. It was a huge storage attic, dimly lit by the natural light coming in from two narrow windows—the same shape and size of all the other windows on this floor.

She ducked through the short doorway and surveyed piles of boxes, old trunks, abandoned furniture and tools, all covered with a thick layer of dust. Any effort to tread lightly through the space, to avoid stirring up clouds of dirt was futile. Her nose objected violently, sending her into a sneezing fit.

Pepper opened one of the large trunks resting on the floor, and was delighted to find it crammed full of colorful and elegant vintage clothing. As far as she was concerned, she had discovered a gold mine. She "oohed" and "aahed" as she pulled each piece of clothing from the treasure chest. The items, created during the mid-nineteen twenties and thirties, must have been left behind by the original owners of the home.

The fabrics were fine silks, brocades, chiffons and satins, and beautifully hand-stitched. She was in fashion design heaven, examining the flow and lines of each garment; obviously couture clothing from France, with hand sewn labels from several French designers.

She desperately longed for a camera to record the fashions or even a sketch pad to make notes, as creative inspiration whirled in her brain. Maybe she could purchase the clothing from the hotel owner. This was a magnificent find.

After searching through a few more trunks, Pepper stood up, trying to shake some of the dust off her dress, and sending her nose into yet another sneezing frenzy. While making her way back through the scattered debris, her foot caught on a throw rug on the floor. She stumbled forward, grabbing onto a broken dining room chair to keep from falling. While inspecting the offending rug, she noticed the edge of a wooden hatch in the floor.

"What have we got here?" she asked, as her "Alice in Wonderland" journey continued. She pulled back the rug and tried to lift the handle on the hatch, but it was locked into place by a sliding bolt on either side. She released the latches and raised the heavy door.

A set of wooden steps led down to a room on the floor below. Fluorescent lights illuminated the space, which appeared to be a large storage closet. Could it be the linen and toiletry supplies for the hotel guest rooms? She crept cautiously down the first few steps, scanning the area to make sure she was alone. The coast was clear, so she continued down to the bottom of the steps.

The staircase hugged the wall at the back of a large, but windowless, claustrophobic space with only one metal door as an entrance. And the temperature in the room was freezing. The air conditioning thermostat must have been set for "meat locker," she thought, as she shivered and goose bumps rippled along her exposed arms.

The room was jammed with row after row of industrial metal shelving, stacked with various sizes of wooden and metal boxes. The lid on one of the long wooden boxes was ajar, so she peeked inside. It was filled with brand new machine guns; their manufacturing tags still attached.

"My God!" she exclaimed, dropping the lid like a hot coal. "What are these doing in a hotel?" She scanned the labels on the hundreds of boxes stacked several deep on each shelf. The word "Ammo" was stamped on the outside of most. She gasped when she read the label, "C-4". "This isn't a linen closet," she said. "This is an arsenal!" I've got to tell Peter, she thought, dashing back down the aisle toward the steps.

Before she made it halfway down the aisle, however, the metal door opened wide, and a heavyset man stepped inside, carrying a large box full of empty shell casings. He spotted the tall, brunette immediately. Her colorful print dress stood out in sharp contrast against the drab military green surroundings.

"What are you doing in here?" he cried, tossing the box aside and making a dash for Pepper. The casings spilled all over the floor, so instead of running forward, he was slipping and sliding over hundreds of round metal cylinders rolling around under his feet. The terrified Pepper began rocking and rolling as well, as she tried desperately to reach the stairs.

Trembling with fear, she finally managed to hop up onto the first step, out of the treacherous footing below, but the man's longer strides had closed the gap between them. He grabbed her long hair and jerked her back down onto the floor.

Pepper screamed in pain, as she fell backwards, landing on her butt. The casings were slippery underfoot, but downright painful when her bottom hit the concrete floor covered with the bumpy metal cylinders. She screamed again; this time not just from the pain, but in anger.

She spun around on the floor and began kicking her attacker with her high-heeled shoes—stabbing him in the chest, the gut, the face—anywhere she could land a blow. He tried frantically to grab her feet, but they were moving too fast.

Her last blow caught him above one eye, and he yelped in pain. Pepper scrambled up the stairs and slammed the hatch shut. She tried desperately to slide the latches back into place, but her attacker began banging on the door below, and she couldn't force them into position.

She scanned the attic for something heavy to move on top of the door. Her only option was a large metal trunk close by. Maybe if she slid it on top and sat on it, she could keep the man from getting through.

She kept one foot on top of the hatch while pulling on the heavy trunk, but the man managed to sneak his hand under the hatch door and grab her around the left ankle. Pepper lost her footing and toppled forward onto the dusty floor. Gagging and coughing from the cloud of dust swirling around her, she kicked frantically with her right foot, trying to get free again. The hatch flew open just as she managed to stab the heel of her shoe into the hand that held her ankle.

Once again, the man screamed in pain and released her. Pepper scooted forward on hands and knees, scampering across the floor like a sand crab on the beach, finally managing to stand up and make a run for the attic door. She squeezed through the opening, back into the bedroom closet and slammed the attic door. But the key was gone.

What had she done with the damned key? It wasn't in the door. It must have fallen out when she opened the door, and now it was on the floor, hidden somewhere under a pile of Styrofoam peanuts. "To hell with it!" she cried, and she ran screaming from her bedroom out into the hallway.

When Agent Harriet Blair heard the screams, she ran out into the hallway, with her gun drawn, and came face-to-face with the dust-covered Pepper. Her formerly shiny brunette tresses were now white with dust, as was every other part of her body and clothing. Only her terrified violet eyes were visible under the thick layer of dirt.

"Pepper?" asked Harriet.

"Don't shoot!" cried Pepper, holding up both hands. "It's me, and I'm being followed!"

Harriet turned and faced the entrance to Pepper's room just as the man from the third floor storage room tumbled out into the hallway.

"Don't move!" she yelled, pointing her gun at yet another dust-covered figure.

At this point, everyone on the floor came running out into the hallway, alerted by Pepper's screams and Harriet's commands.

"What the hell?" asked Peter, looking from one dust-covered vision to the other, as Jason stood behind him trying to stifle a laugh.

"He's part of the arms dealer's group," said Pepper, gasping for breath after her frantic escape, and trying futilely to wipe the dust from her eyes and mouth. "They have a storage room filled with weapons and ammunition down on the third floor. It's connected to the attic on this floor."

Peter called for prisoner transportation, as Harriet hand-cuffed the Applewhite associate and led him toward the elevator.

"Okay," said Peter, trying to figure out how these spice women managed to get themselves into so much trouble and still come out looking like heroes, "show me this room."

Pepper frowned. She really didn't want to go back through that dusty space, but after glancing down at her one-of-a-kind designer frock, realized she couldn't possibly get any dirtier. "Follow me," she replied, leading Peter and Jason into the bedroom closet and squeezing through the attic door.

Peter shook his head in disbelief, as he glanced at Jason. Jason just smiled and shrugged. But after making their way through the attic and down into the storage room, they were both stunned at the sight of the well-stocked arsenal.

"How did my deputies miss this room during their search for the murder weapon?" asked Jason.

They opened the huge metal door and stepped out into the hallway. The outside of the door was covered by a panel that matched the wall perfectly. It was practically invisible unless you knew it was there.

"I wonder what else Applewhite is hiding in this hotel?" asked Peter. "And more importantly, is Clinton Tate aware of what's going on here?"

When Pepper returned to the fourth floor, Ginger and Cinnamon stood staring at her, wondering how on earth to attack such a mess. They escorted the shaken Pepper to the bathroom and stripped off her filthy clothing.

"You might as well burn it," she said, sadly surveying the damage. Not only was her designer creation covered in grime, it was torn where she snagged it on the metal trunk in the attic. She sighed and stepped into the shower under a warm spray of water; then lathered her body from head to toe with a wonderful handmade lavender scented soap.

It was remarkable how this simple act of washing away the dirt also helped cleanse her spirit, as well. She felt one hundred percent better as she toweled off her squeaky clean, lavender scented body and hair.

"There's just one problem," said Cinnamon. "You have no clothes."

Pepper smiled as she remembered the beautiful gowns she found in the trunk in the attic, but unfortunately they would be a tad musty after being stored for seventy or eighty years.

"Maybe Harriet could help," suggested Ginger, leaning out the bedroom door to call for the agent.

"What is it, ladies?" asked Harriet, giving a thumb's up sign at the marked improvement in Pepper's hygiene.

"Pepper needs some clothes," replied Ginger.

"Could we get someone to bring me an outfit from home?" asked Pepper.

"Unfortunately not," said Harriet. "This arms dealer knows the F.B.I. is here, now that we've raided his arsenal; but they don't know that Ginger is still here, as well as you and Cinnamon. We can't have them following one of our agents to your house and back. I'll have someone buy you an outfit. What size do you wear?" she asked, surveying the tall, thin woman.

"Size two," said Pepper.

"Somehow I figured that's what you were going to say," sighed Harriet, regretting her own recent advance into a double-digit clothing size. She really needed to get to the gym more often, she thought, but she was approaching forty and it seemed to get harder each year to keep the pounds at bay.

Ginger sympathetically read Harriet's thoughts, "Just wait until you reach your fifties, dear."

After Peter and Jason returned from the third floor arsenal, Peter called for backup to haul off the weapons in Applewhite's secret stash. It was approaching five o'clock, so Jason bid good-bye to the spice ladies and headed back to the office to wait for his deputies to deliver Henry Jamison for questioning. It was going to be a long night.

* * * * * * * * * * *

Since Henry Jamison was traveling without luggage, he by-passed the luggage pick-up area when he arrived at Hobby Airport and went directly to the rental car booth. So far so good, he thought. He might just manage to pull this off.

As he approached the airport exit, however, he spotted two Sheriff's deputies standing close by. They also spotted Henry. "Damn," he cried. "How did they find me?" He turned and ran in the opposite direction, hoping to disappear into the noisy, crowded airport, dodging groups of passengers clogging the baggage area, anxiously anticipating the arrival of their luggage, and clusters of family members and friends hugging each other in happy reunions.

In a last ditch effort to lose the deputies, he ducked into the men's room and removed his dark jacket, hoping the change of clothing would throw them off his trail. He retrieved a baseball cap from his flight bag and slapped it over his perfectly-styled hair, then shoved his flight bag up under the sinks to further lighten his load. With the cap pulled low over his eyes, he sauntered out of the restroom at a leisurely pace, and joined a large group of tourists with a rolling caravan of luggage.

Henry managed to exit the noisy, bustling airport, following closely behind the crowd of boisterous travelers. They all stopped at the pedestrian traffic light before crossing the roadway to the parking garage. Henry barely felt the blade of the knife as it jabbed into his back at an upward angle underneath his ribs. But he did feel his lung collapse, preventing him from making a sound. When the light turned green, the group of travelers hurried across the street, leaving Henry behind, in a crumpled heap on the sidewalk.

Chapter Twelve

The remaining members of the McCormick family were elated after Sheriff Winters told them Ginger, Cinnamon and Pepper were safe—hidden away at The Grand Hotel under the watchful eye of the F.B.I.

They were, however, concerned about how long this siege would last. How long would they have to wait before they saw their loved ones again? When would this monster, Applewhite, be captured so the residents of Clearwater could feel safe?

Sage was at her wits end. She and her sisters had done everything they could think of to find Maybelle's killer, but it wasn't enough. He was still out there, stalking her mother. Hell, they were all prey to this evil monster, she thought, pacing back and forth on the family room rug. Waiting wasn't her strong suit. She was used to taking action and being in control.

Mace and Curry glanced at each other, concerned about her agitated state.

"Sage, we just have to be patient," said Mace. "Jason will catch Applewhite soon. And Agent Dalton is taking care of your mother and sisters."

His words put a stop to her pacing. She hadn't intended to add to her father's distress, the poor man had been attacked himself just a few hours ago. She just needed an outlet for her pent up frustration.

Ask and ye shall receive. The phone rang. It was Ginger's business line in the office adjacent to the family room. All three McCormick's stared at each other. It hadn't occurred to them during this crisis that Ginger's clients couldn't cancel a year's worth of wedding plans just because their wedding consultant was temporarily out of pocket.

"What should we do?" asked Curry.

"Answer it," replied Sage.

Curry picked up the receiver. "Hello," she said, timidly, and then jerked the receiver away from her ear, as the sounds of a female voice wailed, blubbered and screeched an incomprehensible string of words.

Sage and Curry stared at each other helplessly, as Mace backed out of the room, heading for cover.

"Here," said Curry, handing the receiver to Sage, her fearless leader. "You take it—you're better at confrontations."

Sage glared at her and snatched the phone. "This is Sage McCormick. May I help you?"

"This is Brenda Collins. Where is Ginger?"

"Ginger was in an accident yesterday, and she's unavailable at the moment." That was an understatement. "Is there a problem, Brenda?"

"A problem?" screeched Brenda. "I'll say there's a problem. My wedding starts in three hours. Ginger was supposed to be here at the dock at 3:30 to receive and distribute all my flowers. It's now 3:45. Where is she? I need her to help me with my veil before the photographer arrives at 5:00 to start taking pictures. One hundred and fifty guests will be boarding the Dixie Queen paddle wheeler at Pier Eight at 6:00, and the boat leaves the dock at 6:30, when the ceremony begins."

Sage's eyes had widened with each new revelation as Brenda ticked off the evening's scheduled events. She waved frantically at Curry and whispered, "Find the Collins file!"

Curry dropped to the floor in front of the desk file drawer and flipped through the neatly organized and labeled folders. She plopped the two-inch thick file on top of the desk.

Sage gasped at the sight. The documentation for her criminal cases wasn't this thick. She opened the folder and scanned the contents. Every detail for the entire event was carefully logged: the wedding attire, the flowers, the music, all the wedding vendors, the guest list—even the reception seating charts.

At the very front was a neatly typed schedule for the entire wedding, listing the exact minute each activity occurred from handing out the flowers, to starting the wedding march, to the couple's first dance, to the cake cutting and ending with the bouquet toss. Bless you, Mother. Sage and Curry scanned the list and nodded, smiling at each other. They could do this.

"Okay, Brenda, we've got you covered. My sister, Curry and I will be there in...twenty minutes."

Curry screeched, looking down at her bath robe, and then ran up the stairs to get ready. She kept extra clothes at her parents' house, so she didn't have to haul them back and forth to Houston when she visited. And, since clothes were her business, she had outfits galore.

She threw on a one-of-a-kind, flowing silk dress, stepped into a pair of matching heels, and quickly dabbed make-up foundation over her more visible explosion injuries. She was ready with minutes to spare; her trendy designer handbag clasped around her tiny waist. "Hands free," she joked, scooping up the file folder on the way out.

Sage grabbed her handbag and off they went, but not very far. Sage's cell phone rang as they stepped off the front porch.

"Sage, this is Cynthia Jamison," sobbed the distraught young woman.

"Cynthia, what's wrong?"

"I have to talk to you. I found something in Mother's closet when I was picking out the clothes for her funeral." Cynthia broke down into more sobbing. Sage looked at Curry, not knowing what to do.

"Can I stop by tomorrow morning to talk to you?"

"No, Sage. You have to come now. I know who killed Mother!"

Sage stopped dead in her tracks. This she couldn't ignore. "Did you call Jason?"

"No. I can't. It's about my father. I can't call the police. It's bad, Sage. I need your help."

"Okay, Cynthia. I'll be there in ten minutes. Just hold on." Sage hung up her phone and stared at Curry. "That was Cynthia. She says she found out who killed Maybelle, but she needs to talk to me now."

"Go," urged Curry. "Go now. I can handle this wedding by myself. With Mother's layout, a moron could do it. Just go!"

Sage jumped into her car and sped off to meet Cynthia. Curry, remembering that her car was now a crumpled mass of charred metal, clomped back into the house in search of car keys. Jason had managed to return Cinnamon's SUV, so she snagged those keys and headed for the pier.

She parked next to the huge paddle wheel boat at Pier Eight. The Dixie Queen circled Pelican Bay for daytime tours and formal evening dinner/dance cruises. It was a popular choice for wedding sites, as well, if you could afford the steep price.

Curry was right about Ginger's detailed instructions; following the wedding schedule was a snap. Her mother should write a book called "Weddings for Dummies." Of course, there was probably one on the market already, but she was sure Ginger's version would be better.

She handed out bouquets to one bride and six bridesmaids; then pinned boutonnières and corsages onto one groom, six groomsmen, four ushers, two mothers, two dads, four grandmothers and a partridge in a pear tree—she was about to lose it over the corsage pin scenario. Fortunately, every floral arrangement was labeled, so it was a no-brainer.

Next, Curry moved on to help the bride with her veil and even managed to make some minor improvements, using her fashion design expertise.

The ceremony was held on the upper deck of the boat, just as the sun was setting. It cast a beautiful orange glow on the sparkling blue water in the bay. Curry was positive this gorgeous light show was all part of Ginger's masterful plan. The ceremony went off without a hitch, except for the two flower girls who got into a tug of war over the flower basket halfway down the aisle and had to be separated twice during the vows.

After the ceremony, everyone progressed to the reception in the main ballroom for an extravagant buffet and ear-deafening dance music. The ballroom was packed to maximum capacity, which made Curry a bit nervous. Since she wasn't a very good swimmer, being out on a boat in deep water was a scary proposition. She scanned the area surreptitiously for life jackets—just in case.

As she threaded her way through the tightly packed tables and chairs, someone grabbed her arm and pulled her over to one of the tables. It was a middle-age woman, wearing a gold lamé evening gown. Curry blinked as the dance floor spotlights glinted off the shiny fabric.

"Honey, where did you get that gorgeous dress?" the woman asked in a slow, Southern drawl.

"It's an original," replied Curry. "I designed it myself."

The woman gasped. "A fashion designer right here in Clearwater?"

"Actually, my parents live here, but my boutique is in Houston."

"I have simply got to have an original gown for my daughter's wedding next summer. Where is your shop?"

"It's in the Rice Village area, close to..." The woman's eyes glazed over. She obviously wasn't familiar with Houston. "Why don't you give me your name and number, and I'll call you."

The woman pulled out a card and began to write a phone number on the back.

"I've actually been thinking about moving our shop here," added Curry.

"Oh, sweetie, that's a wonderful plan. You'd be busier than a one-armed paper hanger."

Curry had no response to that statement.

"Now you call me next week, you hear, sugar?"

Curry winked and gave the woman a thumbs-up sign; then headed over to talk to the D.J. about the bride and groom's music list and the upcoming announcement for the cake cutting event.

On her way back to the buffet tables, she caught a glimpse of Clinton Tate, hidden in the shadows at the back of the dimly-lit ballroom. He was in an animated conversation with a short, plump, dark-haired man, and appeared to be somewhat distressed.

Apparently, things weren't going very well for Clinton these days, especially since his wife decided to divorce him and take half his assets. It probably left him a little short on cash. Curry wondered what effect that would have on his Costa Rica project. Could Clinton be the arms dealer the F.B.I. was looking for? She shivered involuntarily at the thought, but hated to pass up the opportunity for a bit of investigating. It was highly unlikely that they would have access to Clinton Tate again.

Curry sauntered past the two men, pretending to check on the wedding guests, and then ducked behind the heavy velvet curtain separating the ballroom from the coat room. She stood next to the curtain, at about the same spot where she thought they were standing, hoping to eavesdrop on their conversation. Unfortunately, the music, laughter and constant chatter in the room drowned out their voices.

When the music stopped, she heard Clinton say, "I need more time. I'm sure Henry Jamison will come through."

"Jamison is history," said the dark-haired man, with a heavy Spanish accent. "You get another partner soon or this deal is finished."

Curry had no idea what they were talking about, but the tone in their voices was frightening. She scurried along the curtain to return to the ballroom and ran right smack dab into Clinton Tate.

"Been here long?" he sneered.

Curry froze like a deer in headlights. She turned around abruptly and began rummaging through the coats hung on a nearby rack. "I was just getting a wrap for my aunt. She's elderly and gets chilled easily." She grabbed a jacket off one of the hangers and dashed out of the coat room, followed by Clinton's suspicious glare.

Running into the kitchen area, she leaned against the counter, gasping for air. Her whole body trembled with fear. How could she be so stupid? Clinton Tate might very well be a murderer, and he had caught her red-handed.

"Are you all right?" asked the caterer. "Can I get you some water?"

"No, I'm fine," she replied, even though her knees were still shaking.

For the rest of the evening, she planned to stay well away from Clinton Tate.

* * * * * * * * * *

Sage slammed her foot down on the accelerator and drove like a bat out of hell toward the Jamison house. She hated to leave Curry alone, facing an irate bride and a boatload of wedding guests, but she needed to talk to Cynthia Jamison.

What had Cynthia found to identify Maybelle's killer? What had the Congressman done that was so terrible she couldn't tell the Sheriff? It was nearly four o'clock, and Sage knew Jason was sending some deputies to pick up Henry Jamison at the airport around five. It would take them about half an hour to get back to Clearwater, so she should have plenty of time to talk to Cynthia before they arrived.

She pulled into the driveway at the Jamison house and hurried up to the front door. The heartbroken Cynthia, still crying, led Sage into the front sitting room.

"It's all here in Dad's journal," she sobbed. "He...he...Oh, Sage, I just can't believe it. My own father is a traitor!"

"A traitor?" asked Sage.

"Yes. Look for yourself." Cynthia shoved a thin hardback notebook into Sage's hands.

Sage opened the book and began to read. She gasped after reading just a few paragraphs. "Oh, my God!" After a few pages, she looked up, "Applewhite," she said. "He's the one the F.B.I. is looking for. Does the journal say who he is?"

Before Cynthia could reply, the front windows were shattered by hundreds of bullets blasting at lightning speed from machine guns. Sage hit the floor, but Cynthia stood, frozen in place, screaming in terror, as bullets pierced the surrounding walls and furniture.

"Get down!" yelled Sage. But Cynthia was hysterical—she couldn't stop screaming. Sage lunged at her, tackling her to the ground, but she continued to scream. "Be quiet, Cynthia," ordered Sage, clamping a hand firmly over her terrified friend's mouth. By the time Sage managed to get Cynthia quiet, the gunfire had stopped, leaving her ears ringing from the deafening sound of the gun blasts.

Sage listened for sounds that someone might be entering the house, but heard nothing. She sat up and peeked out through the shattered front windows. There was no one in sight. "They must have been in a moving vehicle when they fired the bullets," she said. Cynthia bolted off the floor, running for the front door.

"No!" screamed Sage. "Wait..." But before she could get another word out, the barrage of bullets started again. This time, Cynthia crouched down and crawled over to Sage, sobbing hysterically, but at least she wasn't screaming.

They stayed face down on the floor, covering their heads from the flying debris until the ear-splitting gunfire stopped again.

"Let's try to crawl down the hall to the back door," said Sage. "But keep your body as close to the floor as you can."

Cynthia nodded and scooted out into the entryway. Sage spotted the journal on the floor beside her. She grabbed it and stuck it into the waistband of her skirt. Slowly they slid along the polished wooden floor, past the staircase and powder room toward the kitchen at the back of the house.

Before they reached the opening to the kitchen, a bottle came crashing through the glass in the back door, exploding into flames on the kitchen floor.

Both women screamed and scurried back into the entry hall beside the staircase. Black smoke billowed from the flames spreading rapidly along the floor. Sage glanced up at the stairs, but rejected the idea of going up to the second floor, when the first floor would be engulfed in flames in a matter of minutes.

Smoke began to fill the rooms, as they coughed and gasped for air. They had to get out now, but the front door was not an option. The gunmen might decide to make another strafing run.

"In there," yelled Sage, pushing Cynthia toward the powder room across from the staircase. They scooted into the bathroom and closed the door behind them. Sage grabbed a few towels and started shoving them underneath the door to block the smoke. Damn! She realized she had left her purse, along with her cell phone in the sitting room.

The heat from the fire was almost unbearable in the tiny space. The paint on the door began to crack from the flames licking the other side. The only window in the bathroom was a large octagonal stained glass window over the toilet. It was their only way out. Sage picked up a large bronze vase off the vanity and stepped up onto the toilet seat.

"Oh, God," cried Cynthia. "Mother paid $10,000 for that window. It's an antique."

Sage gave her a "you can't be serious" look. "Cover your eyes," she yelled, and she swung the vase as hard as she could, smashing the beautiful glass to smithereens. They leaned their heads out the window, desperately filling their lungs with fresh air.

"You go first," said Sage, carefully placing a towel over the jagged glass at the base of the window.

Cynthia climbed up on the toilet seat, placing her hands on the bottom of the window. She leaned out, head first, while Sage held her ankles, lowering her as close to the ground as she could before letting go. Cynthia dropped three feet onto the ground and rolled to a stop at the edge of the side yard fence.

"Hurry, Sage," she cried.

Sage climbed up on the toilet seat. The towels underneath the door caught fire and smoke began pouring into the room. Since she didn't have anyone to boost her up to the window, she stepped over to the vanity, then up into the window, balancing on the edge while she turned around and backed out.

She grabbed hold of the top of the window frame and dropped down, dangling in mid-air. It was another five-foot drop to the ground. But before she let go, two strong hands grabbed her around the waist and lifted her gently to the ground. She knew who it was before she even turned around; recognizing the familiar, warm scent of his aftershave.

"Are you all right, Sage?" asked Jason, holding her close.

She welcomed the strength and safety of his embrace. "I am now," she said.

Chapter Thirteen

A man wearing dark sunglasses, sitting in a black sedan that was parked across the street from Maybelle Jamison's house, calmly observed the chaotic scene. Sirens and flashing lights announced the arrival of a string of fire trucks and police vehicles. For the second time in one day, the weary fire fighting crew was called out to battle a raging fire. Their energy and resources were dwindling fast, as they stretched the heavy water hoses across the lawn to begin dousing the flames.

The mysterious stranger watched as Sheriff Winters escorted Sage McCormick and Cynthia Jamison from the side of the house, where they had somehow managed to escape the inferno. This was unfortunate—Applewhite would be furious that his operatives had failed to complete their mission.

The trio paused beside the Sheriff's vehicle, huddled close together for a confidential discussion, barely able to hear over the roar of the searing flames and the powerful water sprays. Sage looked over at Cynthia, who nodded her approval. Then she pulled a small, hardback book from the waistband of her skirt and handed it to the Sheriff.

The man in the black sedan sighed, pulled his cell phone from his pocket and punched in Applewhite's number. "The mission was not successful," he reported. "The Sheriff now has the journal. Your cover has been compromised." He hung up the phone, started his vehicle, and drove off, completely unobserved in the midst of the frantic scene.

* * * * * * * * * *

Sage and Cynthia rode to the Sheriff's office with Jason because both their cars were blocked in the Jamison's driveway by

117

the fire trucks. They sat in dazed silence during the short ride, thankful to be alive. Sage couldn't imagine how Cynthia was holding up under such tragedy. Her mother was murdered, her father's office was bombed, then she discovered that he was conspiring with an arms dealer to steal weapons from the government and sell them to terrorists.

And as if that wasn't enough, she was nearly killed by gunfire and burned in a house fire that destroyed her family's home. How could she stand any more trauma? But there would be more—the final blow was yet to be delivered.

The two young women sat across from the Sheriff in a closed interrogation room, as they explained their frightening ordeal at the hands of Applewhite's associates.

"I found the journal hidden in a shoebox in Mother's closet when I was choosing the clothing for her funeral," explained Cynthia, her emotions now completely numb. "I called Sage because I didn't know what to do."

"I got to the house about four o'clock," added Sage. "I didn't have much time to look at the journal before the gunfire started."

Cynthia frowned, remembering their terror, and tears began to run down both cheeks. Sage reached over and squeezed her hand, offering what little comfort she could, while sending a worried glance at Jason. He nodded, acknowledging her concern to proceed with caution, and paused a moment to read the journal.

"We tried to go out the back door," continued Sage, "but they threw a bottle filled with flammable liquid through the glass. The house caught fire, and we escaped through the bathroom window. Thank God I managed to save the book."

Cynthia nodded. "My father was working with an arms dealer," she cried. "Mother found out and must have confronted the dealer. That's why he killed her. That's why he burned down the house, to destroy that journal and keep his identity hidden."

A deputy knocked on the door of the interrogation room and stepped inside. "I need to talk to you, Sheriff. It's about..." He glanced at Cynthia and back at the Sheriff.

Jason nodded and stepped out into the hallway to confer with the deputy.

"It's Henry Jamison," he said. "He was stabbed at the airport. He's dead."

* * * * * * * * * *

Applewhite hung up the phone after receiving the call from his associate, telling him that Sheriff Winters was now in possession of Henry Jamison's journal. That idiot Jamison and his obnoxious wife had screwed up his entire operation.

Everything had been running smoothly for two years. His group had moved literally tons of weapons to their target in Central America, thanks to Jamison's credentials that opened the gates to the military bases.

It was a brilliant plan that was working like clockwork. Even though Jamison was about to lose his political connections, they still had time to make a few more runs before the leak was plugged—until Maybelle discovered that damned journal.

What in hell was Jamison thinking, putting all those details down in writing? The man's ego was off the chart, but his I.Q. couldn't even measure a blip on the screen. And then, when that bitch showed up telling him to get the hell out of her hotel, he knew his operation was on shaky ground.

At first, he thought he could control the damage by killing her and blaming Glen Durst. But everything began to collapse when Ginger McCormick got caught in the aftermath.

Someone must have been watching their organization if they knew enough to get her tucked away out of his reach. But who? The operative he sent to the McCormick's house said the Sheriff didn't know where she was. That means it wasn't the Sheriff, but another law enforcement agency, probably the F.B.I.

But it didn't matter now. The Sheriff had that journal, naming him as the arms dealer. He would just have to get out of the country for a while, until things calmed down and he could find another greedy sucker to set him up with a cover in the U.S. like Clinton Tate had done.

Then he could start the process all over again. It was just a slight delay—a minor inconvenience. He knew without a shadow of doubt that he could find another pair of accomplices like Henry Jamison and Clinton Tate. Everyone has a price. It's just a matter of finding out what they wanted. Those two wanted piles of money, and he wanted power. It was a fair trade.

But he didn't plan to go quietly. That wasn't his style. His associates had already taken care of Henry Jamison and, thanks to Henry's journal, Clinton Tate would be rotting in a Federal prison for the rest of his life. Applewhite, however, had one more visit to make before he disappeared.

*   *   *   *   *   *   *   *   *   *

Following their interview with Jason, Sage took the distraught Cynthia home with her. When Cynthia received word about her father's death, it was the final blow that sent her into a catatonic state. Sage wasn't about to let her head back to her condo in Houston alone, so she called to let her father know the outcome of the battle at the Jamison's house, and asked him to prepare one of the guest rooms for Cynthia. Grateful for Sage's hospitality, Cynthia collapsed from exhaustion the minute she was guided to her room.

Sage and Mace huddled quietly in the McCormick's cozy, but outdated kitchen, awaiting further word from Jason about how the F.B.I. planned to end this siege.

"Jason thinks Applewhite has probably left the country by now," said Sage, trying to assuage her own fears, as well as her father's.

"They're scattering like rats on a sinking ship," agreed Mace. "Unfortunately, most of them won't be caught and locked up. They'll just go into hiding until they can regroup and start over somewhere else."

Sage nodded. It was sad but true. There was really no way to stop such an evil undercurrent in today's permissive society. Sometimes freedom carries a heavy price.

*   *   *   *   *   *   *   *   *   *

On the fourth floor of The Grand Hotel, Cinnamon was in a cooking frenzy. It was only six o'clock, but she had already prepared enough food for a small army. Not only were the current six residents set for dinner that evening, but midnight snack binges and lunch the next day, as well.

She couldn't help it. She was going stir crazy holed up in this elegant prison. Her restaurant workdays were non-stop, twelve-hour marathons. Lounging around a hotel room for hours on end was worse than torture.

Agent Dalton stuck his head into the small, but well-equipped kitchen and sniffed the fragrant mixture of aromas. There was a delectable-looking chocolate confection cooling on the counter, some heavenly garlic rolls baking in the oven, a plump chicken in the rotisserie, and a large pot of beef soup bubbling on the stove.

"Expecting company, are you?" he asked, surveying the mountain of food.

"You can never have enough food," she replied, stirring the simmering soup.

"Smells delicious," he said, inhaling the aroma from the pot. "But I think it could use a little thyme."

Cinnamon glared at him. "Mother told me you're a pretty good chef," she admitted. "But you know what they say about too many cooks."

Peter smiled. "Just a suggestion," he added, turning to leave the kitchen.

Cinnamon carefully tasted the soup and glanced over at the kitchen door. She stomped over to the huge, built-in refrigerator, opened the vegetable bin and pulled out a bag of fresh thyme. Next, she stripped off the tiny, fragrant leaves and sprinkled a few into the soup, stirring for a moment, then nodded her approval and dumped in the rest.

Standing just outside the kitchen door, Peter smelled the aroma of the steaming herbs and chuckled, "A woman after my own heart." His cell phone rang. It was Jason.

"Peter," he said. "We've got a real hornet's nest here. Sage McCormick and Cynthia Jamison were attacked by some kind of terrorist group at the Jamison house this afternoon. I'm sure they were part of Applewhite's organization. We're talking machine-gun fire and Molotov cocktails. The house pretty much destroyed by fire, but Sage and Cynthia managed to escape, along with a journal that belonged to Henry Jamison. He recorded all the details about his involvement with Applewhite."

"Does it say who Applewhite is?" asked Peter anxiously.

"Yeah, it's Gordon Ellis. He's part of a group of arms dealers in Costa Rica. He hooked up with Clinton Tate down there. For a large fee, Clinton let Gordon operate his arms business out of the hotel. He also set up the arrangement between Henry and Gordon to steal weapons from military bases."

"We knew it was someone here in the hotel," admitted Peter. "We just didn't know who. And we suspected Clinton Tate was connected. His project in Costa Rica was moving along faster than usual. He had to be getting some kind of kick backs. What about Henry Jamison?"

"He's dead," replied Jason. "They got to him at Hobby Airport before my deputies did."

"I'll get an arrest warrant for Gordon Ellis," said Peter. "He's probably long gone by now. My guess is he's got a sack full of fake passports, so he can go in and out of the country at will. But we'll put out the word anyway."

"That's all we can do," agreed Jason.

After ordering the arrest warrants for Gordon Ellis and Clinton Tate, Peter and Agent Ted Johnson left Agent Harriet Blair in charge of the "prisoners" on the fourth floor, while they headed down to the restaurant kitchen to look for Gordon. They assumed that their search would be futile, but they had to make the effort.

*   *   *   *   *   *   *   *   *   *

Gordon and two of his associates waited patiently in a hidden alcove off the main lobby, as they watched the elevator doors. Gordon knew it was just a matter of time before the Sheriff contacted the group of lawmen who were still holding Ginger McCormick on the fourth floor, and his patience was soon rewarded when two men dressed in dark suits, obviously F.B.I., exited the elevator.

Now was his chance. Gordon planned to take a little extra insurance along for his foreign trip, just in case he ran into any problems. His two associates, dressed as waiters, pushing food carts, entered the elevator and used their key to get to the fourth floor.

Gordon went around behind the hotel office to a hidden closet which housed the express elevator, installed for the private residence. As his helpers overtook any guards posted at the main elevator, he planned to sneak in the back way. This elevator opened out into the butler's pantry behind the fourth floor kitchen.

Gordon much preferred surprise attacks to frontal assaults. They usually required less effort on his part. He planned to snatch Ginger and walk out the back door of the hotel where his associates would be waiting for him in a van. Unfortunately, he hadn't figured on three spices instead of one.

When the elevator doors opened into the butler's pantry, he was caught off guard by the delicious aromas of cooking food. He stepped into the kitchen just as Cinnamon turned around to place a pan of fresh baked rolls on the counter.

"Gordon," she said, smiling. "What are you doing up here?"

"I...came up to check on you," he stammered, doing some quick back-pedaling to adjust his initial plan. What the hell was Cinnamon doing here? Was the F.B.I. babysitting the entire McCormick family?

"Did Peter send you up for another opinion about my cooking?"

Gordon paused. Peter must be one of the agents. "It smells like you're doing a damned fine job on your own. Are you trying to take over my job?"

"You're a great instructor, Gordon, but I've got a long way to go before I'm as good a chef as you are."

"You're just being modest," countered Gordon, reaching into his pocket for his gun. He had already revised his plan. It didn't matter to him which spice he took; as far as he was concerned, Cinnamon was just as good as Ginger.

* * * * * * * * * *

As Gordon was on the way to the top floor of the hotel, Pepper and Ginger were waiting impatiently in the front sitting room for dinner.

"I'm starving," said Pepper. "Cinnamon has been torturing us all evening with those tantalizing cooking smells. I'm going to go check on dinner."

"Bring me a snack if it's going to be much longer," asked Ginger. "I'm hungry, too."

Pepper stepped out of the room into the hallway just in time to see the main elevator doors closing. Two men had just dragged an unconscious Harriet Blair onto the elevator. She gasped and backed up into the sitting room.

"What's wrong?" asked Ginger, frightened by Pepper's expression.

"Two men just took Harriet down in the elevator. She was unconscious, or..."

"Where's Peter?" asked Ginger, "and Ted?"

"I don't know," replied Pepper. They stared at each other in terror, trying to decide what to do.

"Let's get Cinnamon and try to find Peter," said Ginger.

Pepper nodded and they crept slowly out into the hallway, carefully scanning each room as they inched along. The entire floor appeared to be empty except for the voices coming from the kitchen. The two women paused outside the kitchen door, and Pepper peeked inside.

"It's Gordon," she whispered to Ginger.

Ginger frowned. "Peter wouldn't let Gordon come up here."

Inside the kitchen, Cinnamon was beginning to feel uncomfortable about Gordon's sudden appearance. "How did you get into the butler's pantry?" she asked.

"There's a private express elevator for this floor. It's the same way we'll be leaving here," he smiled, pointing his gun at Cinnamon.

She froze on the spot, but her brain didn't freeze. It was racing, desperately trying to find a way out of this nasty situation. Gordon must be the arms dealer operating under cover at the hotel. Posing as a chef? Hell, he wasn't posing, he really was a chef, and a damned good one, too. Apparently the pay was better for an arms dealer, she reasoned, but the consequences could really suck. She quickly scanned the counter, looking for a weapon.

"Don't even think about it," warned Gordon, anticipating her plan. It definitely would have been easier to nab the Mother, he thought. He knew how resourceful and tricky Cinnamon could be.

Outside in the hallway, Pepper gasped when she saw Gordon's gun. "He must be the hotel employee Peter is looking for. We've got to stop him," she whispered to Ginger.

"You distract him," said Ginger, "and I'll sneak around behind him through the pantry."

Pepper nodded, pressing her body flat against the wall right outside the kitchen door, as Ginger sneaked past and entered the pantry door. Pepper took a deep breath, trying to calm her nerves and shouted, "Cinnamon, when is dinner going to be ready. I'm starving!"

Cinnamon jumped at the sound of Pepper's voice. She couldn't let her sister come into the kitchen. She refused to let Gordon take both of them. "It's almost ready," she replied. "Just be patient and I'll call you."

"Who's that?" asked Gordon.

"Pepper, my sister."

"What is this, a family reunion? Where's Ginger?"

Cinnamon shrugged.

Pepper popped her head through the kitchen door. "Hi, Gordon," she said, smiling cheerfully, while her knees shook uncontrollably.

"Join the party," he said, motioning with his gun for her to come in.

Pepper ran over to Cinnamon, hugging her sister while she whispered into her ear, "Mother is in the pantry."

"Well," sneered Gordon. "It looks like I'm getting two spices for the price of one. But three would be better. I'm not going to ask you again. Where's Ginger?"

The two sisters stared at him in shock, as their diminutive mother approached Gordon from behind, wielding the biggest iron skillet they had ever seen. They were even more amazed at her double-handed, over-head swing as the skillet came crashing down with a powerful, bone-crunching whack onto Gordon's head.

He never even knew what hit him—he just dropped in his tracks. Ginger tossed the skillet on the counter and ran over to hug her daughters.

"Damn, Mother," exclaimed Cinnamon. "You don't mess around!"

"I'm tired of this nonsense," replied Ginger. "I'm going home."

"Wait," said Cinnamon. "We can't just go down the elevator. Gordon's cohorts could be waiting for him. We need to tie him up to make sure he can't get away and then call Peter."

"We can't call anyone," countered Pepper. "Harriet was abducted and Peter took our phones."

"What about him?" asked Ginger, poking Gordon's limp body with her foot. "Do you think he has a phone?"

Cinnamon dropped down on the floor to check Gordon's pockets. "Voila," she said excitedly, retrieving a tiny cell phone. "But, I don't know Peter's number."

"Just call 911," suggested Ginger.

"No," argued Pepper. "The police would arrive with sirens blasting. It would alert Gordon's men and they would escape. There are at least two of them downstairs who took Harriet."

"Then call Jason," said Ginger.

"Do you know his number?" asked Cinnamon.

"Give me that phone," demanded Ginger, impatient to get out of her prison. She punched in Sage's cell phone number. "Sage, this is your mother. Call Jason and tell him to call Peter and tell him Cinnamon, Pepper and I have got Gordon Ellis up here on the fourth floor of the hotel. He's out like a light and trussed up like a goose. And tell them to make it snappy." Click.

*   *   *   *   *   *   *   *   *   *

Sage stared at her cell phone and glanced over at Mace. Then she did exactly as her mother ordered. "Jason, you need to call Peter and tell him to get up to the fourth floor of the hotel. Mother, Cinnamon and Pepper have captured Gordon Ellis. Hurry." Click.

Sage grabbed Mace and pushed him out the door, telling him what had just transpired. They climbed into her Mercedes and Sage screeched out of the driveway, steering with one hand while dialing Curry's cell phone with the other.

Jason knew better than to question Sage's advice. He called Peter immediately. "Get up to the fourth floor now. The spice women have captured Gordon Ellis."

"Damn," said Peter.

"Yeah," agreed Jason.

Chapter Fourteen

Peter raced toward the hotel elevator with Agent Ted Johnson close on his heels. "Get me some back up," he yelled into his cell phone. "I need a net thrown over this hotel now! I don't want a single person to leave here." He corralled the extra sheriff's deputies that Jason had assigned to the hotel. "Guard the front and back entrances," he told them, "and check for any vehicles parked close to the building." The deputies scattered in different directions to cordon off the area, as the frightened and restrained hotel guests and restaurant patrons began to clog the lobby.

The two F.B.I. agents jumped into the elevator and inserted the key. "I don't believe it," Peter said. "How did those three manage to subdue Gordon Ellis?"

When the doors opened on the top floor, they dashed down the hall, finding the McCormick women in the kitchen, scarfing down the food Cinnamon had prepared.

"Where's Agent Blair?" asked Peter.

"Two men took her down in the elevator," replied Pepper. "She was unconscious."

"I'll go look for her," offered Ted.

Peter glanced down at Gordon Ellis's limp body, lying on the floor beside the refrigerator. His hands and feet were tied with plastic garbage bags and his gun lay on the kitchen counter.

"He's going to have quite a headache when he wakes up," said Cinnamon.

Ginger grimaced. "I sneaked up behind him and hit him over the head with a skillet," she explained, apologetically.

"That will be the least of his worries, I'm sure," replied Peter, shaking his head in disbelief at their accomplishment. "Thank you, ladies. You have captured one of the top ten criminals on the F.B.I.'s most wanted list."

"The pleasure was all ours," said Cinnamon. "Care for some soup, Agent Dalton?" she winked.

"Maybe later," he smiled. "We've got a few more suspects to round up yet."

* * * * * * * * * *

As Sage sped toward The Grand Hotel, she called Curry to get her up to date on the latest developments in the case.

"Hello," said Curry, screaming into the phone over the noisy dance music and celebrating guests.

Sage jerked the phone away from her ear at the painful blast of noise. "We found out who killed Maybelle," she yelled, so Curry could hear. "It was Gordon Ellis. He's also the arms dealer. Mother, Cinnamon and Pepper have captured him at the hotel. I'm headed there now."

"Gordon Ellis?" shouted Curry. "The chef?"

"Yeah," replied Sage. "And his accomplices were Henry Jamison, who was killed by one of Gordon's associates this afternoon, and Clinton Tate."

"Clinton Tate," repeated Curry. "He's here on the boat. He's with a dark-haired man who has a Spanish accent. They were talking about Henry Jamison earlier."

Sage paused. "You didn't talk to him, did you?" she asked, with mounting concern.

"Well," stalled Curry. "I was sort of eavesdropping on their conversation, and he caught me in the act. But I don't think he's really sure I was listening. He just suspects."

"Stay away from him!" ordered Sage. "Be sure he doesn't catch you alone somewhere."

"That's not likely," admitted Curry. "This boat is packed. There's more danger in the possibility of a sinking ship than being caught alone."

"Just be careful," urged Sage. "I'll let Peter know where Clinton is now, because they've issued a warrant for his arrest, so brace yourself for an F.B.I. invasion."

"Oh, damn," exclaimed Curry. "I've already had enough excitement for one day. I just want to go home and go to bed."

"Hang in there," encouraged Sage. "I'm going to the hotel to get Mother, Cinnamon and Pepper. This whole mess should be over in just a few more hours."

"Good luck," screamed Curry, as the D.J. cranked up the volume for "The Macarena" and a herd of slightly inebriated guests began spilling out onto the dance floor.

*　*　*　*　*　*　*　*　*　*

Sage and Jason brought their respective vehicles to a screeching halt simultaneously at the entrance to the hotel. F.B.I. agents and sheriff's deputies were scouring the grounds in search of Gordon Ellis's fleeing group members and blocking all the exits to prevent their escape. Jason had already alerted Peter to expect their arrival, so Agent Johnson was waiting for Sage, Jason and Mace at the elevator to whisk them up to the fourth floor.

"We've captured the two associates who overpowered Agent Blair," he said. "They were holding her in a van out back, waiting for Gordon to nab Ginger. Your mother knocked Gordon out with a skillet," he chuckled. "She's probably going to get a medal—not to mention a reward. All we need to wind up this case is Clinton Tate."

"I can help you out there," offered Sage. "Right now, he's a wedding guest on the Dixie Queen paddle wheel boat that's cruising around Pelican Bay. Curry saw him talking to a Hispanic man about Henry Jamison just a short while ago."

Agent Johnson smiled. "This is going to be easier than we thought. He can't get far if he's trapped on a boat in the middle of the bay."

When the elevator doors opened, Sage, Mace and Jason were greeted by two F.B.I. agents escorting a hand-cuffed and disoriented Gordon Ellis downstairs to a waiting van. Sage hoped they planned to lock him up and throw away the key. That monster had wreaked havoc on their quiet little community, leaving death and destruction in his wake. Granted, he was enabled by the greed of men like Henry Jamison and Clinton Tate, but Gordon was an evil man, and the innocent victims in Clearwater had paid a high price for his clandestine operation.

Sage ran down the hallway, looking for her mother and sisters, with Mace following close behind. She found them huddled in the kitchen, stuffing their faces with Cinnamon's delectable dinner buffet.

"Mother," she cried, running to hug Ginger.

"Sage, Mace," replied Ginger. The whole family hugged each other, laughing and crying over their joyous reunion.

"Where's Curry?" asked Ginger.

"She's standing in for you at the Collins' wedding," replied Sage.

"Oh, bless her," said Ginger. "In all the chaos, I completely forgot about Brenda. I hope she will forgive me."

"I'm sure she understands. And with your detailed instructions, Curry should do fine."

Ginger smiled. "It pays to be organized."

Sage nodded and hugged her mother again.

Agent Johnson was already conferring with Peter about the whereabouts of Clinton Tate. Peter glanced over at Sage and the other McCormick family members, amazed at their resourcefulness. "What do they need us for?" he asked.

"To transport the bad guys after they collect them," replied Ted.

Peter nodded in agreement and motioned to Jason. "We need to board the Dixie Queen to arrest Clinton Tate," he said. "Any suggestions?"

"I'll radio the Boat Patrol," replied Jason. "They can meet you at Pier 10. We keep four motor boats there for rescues and water patrols. They will contact the captain on the Dixie Queen, and get your agents on board."

"Perfect," said Peter, putting in a call to send out a few agents to the pier.

* * * * * * * * * *

On board the Dixie Queen, Curry tried to maintain her clandestine surveillance of Clinton Tate, but she wasn't taking any chances. The F.B.I. agents were more than capable of handling this mission without her assistance. One scary encounter with Clinton that evening was enough.

Sage had called to let her know that the Boat Patrol planned to ferry three F.B.I. agents out to the paddle wheeler. Curry had no idea how Clinton would react to this turn of events, but hoped the arrest would take place as inconspicuously as possible for the sake of the bride and groom. Law enforcement intervention doesn't exactly make for fond wedding day memories. She kept her fingers crossed that all would proceed quietly, as she watched anxiously through the panoramic picture windows in the ballroom for the agents to arrive.

Curry glanced back at the rambunctious wedding guests and locked eyes with Clinton Tate. He was staring at her with a questioning look. Did he suspect trouble was on the way? Had someone notified him about Henry Jamison's assassination and Gordon's arrest? If that was the case, this scene could turn ugly.

She averted her eyes and moved quickly into a crowd of gyrating dancers, hoping to hide from Clinton's sinister stare. A few minutes later, she saw two F.B.I. agents walk past one of the ballroom windows. Unfortunately, Clinton saw them, too. Now it was his turn to look like a deer caught in headlights. He froze, and then glanced around frantically, trying to choose an escape route.

A third agent entered the ballroom with the boat captain. Clinton pushed his way through the crowd of dancers, dashing toward the ballroom's rear exit that opened out onto the observation deck.

"No!" cried Curry. "He's getting away!" She began to wave her arms in the air wildly, trying to attract the attention of the agent and captain, while pushing her way through the crowd in their direction.

"He's going out the rear door," she yelled. "Follow him."

"Are you Curry?" asked the agent.

"Yes," she replied. "But he's getting way."

"Don't worry," assured the agent. "He's not going to get far on a boat. There are two more agents outside."

But Curry wasn't so sure. They hadn't seen the desperate look on Clinton's face.

"Where is the man he was talking to about Henry Jamison," the agent asked. "Can you point him out to me?"

Curry quickly scanned the faces around the room. "No," she replied. "He's not here."

"Okay," said the agent. "We'll worry about him later."

The agent and boat captain stepped outside onto the deck, which wrapped around the entire ballroom. They hurried toward the back of the boat. Curry followed them, anxious to see what was happening. The cold, damp ocean breeze hit her like an icy blast. She should have grabbed a jacket before leaving the warm ballroom, she thought. Her silk dress whipped wildly around her legs and her long, brown hair blew into her eyes, as she searched the dimly lit deck for signs of Clinton Tate.

As she rounded the side of the ballroom, approaching the observation deck, she spotted the desperate Clinton, cornered against the boat railing by the advancing agents. Suddenly, he climbed up onto the railing and leaped into the chilly water, a good fifteen feet below.

The astonished agents ran to peer over the rail, and the captain radioed the engine room to stop the huge vessel. Curry ran to the rail, searching the churning ocean waves, but it was too dark to see anything. The noise from the water splashing through the huge paddle wheel drowned out the agents' voices, as they shouted to each other.

The patrol boat captain switched on their powerful spotlights, scanning the water for Clinton. Amazingly, he had survived the fall. He swam frantically, trying to escape the pull of the huge paddle wheel, sucking him closer into its range. Paddle boats can't stop on a dime. It would take several minutes before the powerful paddle would stop its forward motion. The spotlight followed Clinton's futile attempt to escape the strong pull, as his body was drawn closer and closer to the blades. Finally, he disappeared underneath the churning foam.

"Where is he?" shouted one agent.

"He's gone," replied another.

"No," cried a deputy from the patrol boat, "he's on the wheel."

Clinton was scooped up by one of the giant blades in the paddle wheel and was slowly rising to the top, just like a Ferris wheel ride. The water-logged fugitive hung on for dear life, as he coughed and sputtered, trying to catch his breath. The huge wheel finally came to a halt, with the exhausted Clinton shivering and sobbing. It was the end of the line for Clinton Tate.

"How in hell are we going to get him down from there?" asked one of the agents.

The only answer, of course, was a helicopter; so the Boat Patrol radioed the Air-Rescue Team, and once again, help was on the way.

By now, the wedding guests were alerted to the daring escape scene and spilled out onto the deck, as the captain made a futile attempt at mob control.

"The show's over, folks," he announced through a hand-held microphone. "Please return to the ballroom."

But the rowdy and rather tipsy crowd wasn't buying this line. Not with a semi-drowned fugitive stuck on top of a paddle wheel and a helicopter bearing down on the scene. This wedding had turned out to be the Mother of all party entertainment. There was no way the captain could pry their icy-cold fingers from that boat rail.

The crowd cheered through chattering teeth as the helicopter hovered overhead, whipping the already brisk ocean breeze into a wind storm. They held their collective breaths as the rescue officer dropped by a thin cable from the aircraft; then sent up a roar of approval as he snagged the freezing Clinton and lifted him safely into the helicopter.

Curry had already retreated into the warmth of the ballroom to grab her jacket, while the rescue scenario was playing out. The boat would soon be headed for the pier, and she was anxious to get home to see her recently freed family members. What a nightmare these past two days had been—it seemed more like a week. She planned to sleep for the next twenty-four hours.

The ballroom was deserted. Even the D.J. had abandoned his post. So much for the bouquet toss, she thought, as she searched the coat rack for her jacket.

"You won't need that where you're going," said a deep male voice with a heavy Spanish accent. "It's quite warm in Central America," he added, pressing the barrel of a gun against her back.

Curry sighed. How could this be happening? Enough is enough, she thought angrily. And I'm not taking any more of this crap! She paused for a moment, planning her strategy, then turned around, flashing him a sultry, sexy smile and batting her long dark eyelashes over her deep violet eyes. The fat little twit was four inches shorter than she was, but the way she leaned in close to his protruding belly, he felt more like Harrison Ford.

She teasingly brushed her fingertips down the front of his shirt. "Well, now," she said, in her best, fake Southern drawl, "that sounds real nice."

But his moment of pleasant surprise was followed immediately by torturous agony, as Curry's right knee slammed with brutal force into his unsuspecting groin. When he doubled over from intense pain, she snatched the fire extinguisher off the wall and whacked him on the head with a violent blow, knocking him out cold. "Don't mess with Texas!" she shouted.

She jerked the drapery cords off the velvet curtain and bound his hands and feet faster than a cowboy tying up a steer in a rodeo. Then she grabbed her jacket, scooped up the man's gun with her handkerchief, and dashed out the ballroom door just as the boat gently bumped the edge of the pier.

"Here," she said, dropping the gun into one of the F.B.I. agent's hands. "Clinton Tate's accomplice is tied up in the coat room. This gun belongs to him."

The agent stood speechless, as he watched the tall, drop-dead gorgeous brunette glide down the gang plank.

Curry was ready to hit the road. It had been an interminably long day, starting off with a bomb blast and ending up with a late-night boat ride with a couple of scary wedding guests. It was way past her bedtime.

Chapter Fifteen

At The Grand Hotel, Special Agent Peter Dalton was winding down the investigation that had all but consumed his life for the past two years. The arms dealer, Applewhite, was in custody, and Peter had just received word that Clinton Tate was arrested, as well.

It had been a long and arduous mission, but they finally succeeded, thanks to the help of a resourceful group of "spice women," in getting one more bad guy off the streets. He was exhausted from the stressful and many times frustrating case, and planned to take a much-needed vacation. After that, he would return to do it all over again. His employment was secured by a never-ending stream of criminals threatening the safety of his beloved country.

Granted, when his mission was accomplished, he always felt a sense of satisfaction that he had made a difference and the world would be a safer place. But he was beginning to grow weary of the prospect of dealing with the criminal element in society on a full-time, long-term basis. It might be time for him to go in a different direction. What that direction might be, he wasn't sure, but he intended to do some serious thinking about it.

As the agents scurried about, packing up their equipment, the McCormick family—all but Curry—prepared to leave the area for their long-awaited journey home. Cinnamon had cleaned up the kitchen area, leaving it sparkling clean and as good as new. All traces of her cooking marathon were either happily consumed by the ravenous fourth-floor guests or returned to the restaurant kitchen.

Pepper called Curry, who was on her way to the hotel after leaving the wedding, and asked her to make a quick side trip to the house to pick up clothing for Ginger and her. Next, she made a valiant effort to scoop up the pile of clingy Styrofoam peanuts and stack the shipping boxes back in the closet where she found them, finding the missing skeleton key in the process. She dropped the key into its envelope and placed it carefully on the top box, so it would be easily accessible when she returned to the attic to retrieve the treasure chest of vintage clothing.

After hearing that Marla Tate was the hotel's new owner, Pepper decided to ask her about purchasing the beautiful garments. They would make a wonderful display in her shop—the new one. The one she planned to open right here in Clearwater, decorated with fashions that were custom-made many years ago for a lucky Clearwater resident.

She knew Curry would agree that it was a good idea. All they needed to do was find the perfect location. It should be in a trendy area, but with a vintage look—Old Towne, of course. And she just happened to know about a vacancy in the area. Actually, it was very vacant. It was the empty shell of the building that formerly housed Congressman Henry Jamison's office. It would take a while to rebuild, but she and Curry could design the building to meet their aesthetic and functional needs perfectly.

Curry arrived at the hotel a short while later, bringing clothes for Ginger and Pepper. Once again, there was a happy family reunion, as they all hugged and talked excitedly about the capture of Gordon Ellis and Clinton Tate.

"I hope Brenda Collins wasn't too upset about my missing her wedding," said Ginger.

"She was very gracious after I explained your situation," replied Curry. "And with your detailed instructions, the wedding went off without a hitch—until Clinton Tate decided to attempt a swan dive off the boat into the bay, that is. But the guests loved it. It was the best entertainment they'd ever encountered at a wedding before."

Ginger shook her head disapprovingly at the thought of such drama interrupting one of her perfectly-planned wedding events. "I'm just glad he wasn't injured."

Ginger and Pepper changed into their newly delivered clothing while Pepper told Curry about the treasure she had discovered in the attic, and asked about the possibility of moving their business to Clearwater.

"I can't wait to see the garments," exclaimed Curry. "Can we go in there now?"

Pepper frowned, looking down at her recently replaced frock. "Maybe we should have someone retrieve the trunk for us. It's a tad dusty in there."

"Are you sure you want to move the boutique to Clearwater? The excitement here over the past two days makes Houston look tame by comparison," said Curry, gently rubbing the cuts on her forehead caused by the office explosion.

"I doubt very seriously that we will have another episode like this in Clearwater," assured Ginger.

Pepper and Curry glanced at each other, remembering their narrow escapes from death. "Nah," said Pepper. "That couldn't happen again in a million years."

"You're right," agreed Curry. "Clearwater is a safe, quiet little town. Our clients would love to come here."

"We could even arrange for them to stay in this hotel," added Pepper. "They would love it here on the bay."

They giggled like two little girls in a candy store. Ginger smiled, thankful that everything had turned out so well—except for poor Maybelle and Henry, of course.

Sage wandered from room to room, impatiently trying to round up her family and herd them toward the elevator. For victims who were so upset about being kidnapped and held captive, they certainly seemed to be taking their own sweet time about leaving.

This had been the absolute worst day of her entire life—starting off with a stressful car chase and ending with a gun battle followed by a house fire. Her nerves were frazzled, she was exhausted, and she wanted to go home—now! But there seemed to be a never-ending stream of details to attend to before this chapter of their lives was finally closed.

Just when Sage thought things might be winding down, the elevator doors opened and an agitated Marla Tate, wearing a blue satin ball gown and a diamond choker, bounded down the hallway. "I need to talk to Cinnamon," she declared, her platinum blonde bouffant hairdo standing on end as if she'd recently received an electric shock. "Where is she?"

Sage sighed, giving up all hope that this circus would be mobile anytime soon. "In there," she said, pointing toward the kitchen.

Marla marched down the hallway, finding Cinnamon in the kitchen with Peter. He was sampling the last of the thyme-flavored soup, as they discussed their culinary preferences.

"Cinnamon," exclaimed the breathless Marla. "You've got to help me. The F.B.I. just hauled off my chef. There's no one to run the kitchen!"

"Help you?" asked Cinnamon.

"Yes, I need you to be my new head chef."

Cinnamon stared at Marla in shock, while Peter beamed. "Head chef?" she asked, trying to grasp the magnitude of Marla's request. "Of a five-star restaurant?" Cinnamon felt dizzy at the mere prospect. Peter pulled up a stool and gently guided her onto the seat.

"Of course she will," he said. "She's the best chef this side of the Mississippi."

Cinnamon frowned, looking at him liked he'd lost his mind. It takes years to reach the level of head chef in a restaurant with that kind of rating. She had been a professional chef for only four years. "I don't think I have the experience you're looking for, Marla. I'll be glad to help you out until you can find another head chef. I can even recommend a few you might want to recruit."

"But I want you," pleaded Marla. "I've been to your restaurant in Houston and tasted your cooking. You grew up here in Clearwater, and I know your family. I can't take a chance on hiring another stranger like Clinton did. That was a disaster! I need you, Cinnamon. Please say you'll be my head chef."

Cinnamon looked at Peter for guidance, while weighing the consequences of her decision. Head chefs at a five-star restaurant were held to a higher standard—she didn't want to make that leap too soon, ruin her career, and wind up as a short-order cook in a fast food joint.

Peter smiled sympathetically, trying to lend support, but understanding her uncertainty. He was facing the same dilemma— leaving a familiar, comfortable career for the unknown. "Go for it," he said.

Cinnamon smiled, took a deep breath, and turned to Marla. "Okay, I'll give it a shot."

"Wonderful!" exclaimed Marla. "I'll meet you in the kitchen tomorrow morning at seven with your contract. We do brunch at ten on Sundays. I hope you've got some innovative ideas because I plan to spice things up around here. It's been far too boring for me," she added, as she sailed down the hallway toward the elevator.

Innovative ideas? Spice things up? Now that's a person who understands me, thought Cinnamon. Ideas were popping into her head like crazy. She couldn't stop them even if she wanted to, and was sure she'd be up all night planning an entire new menu. She hoped Marla meant what she said, because Cinnamon knew how to spice things up.

She was still floating with joy when her family came to collect her. They were all excited about her good news. Then Curry and Pepper announced their plans to move their boutique to Clearwater.

"Now, we just have to figure out a way to get Sage to move here, too," said Ginger, "and then we'll be one big happy family again."

"Not likely," replied Sage. "At least, not any time in the near future," she added, with a quick glance in Jason's direction.

Peter's cell phone rang and he stepped into his office to take the call. "Special Agent Dalton," he answered, and then paused while the caller spoke. "Yes," he replied, "Gordon Ellis, code name Applewhite." (pause) "You're kidding." (pause) "How much?" (pause) "Damn, I'll tell them. Thanks, Anderson."

Peter caught up with the McCormick family members as they waited for the elevator. "I just received some good news," he told them. "Apparently the government issued a reward last year for the capture of Gordon Ellis. It's still in effect and, Ginger, you, Cinnamon and Pepper qualify for the money."

The family members stared at each other, not quite sure how to respond. Sage finally broke the silence, "Bounty hunters!" she cried. "It could be a whole new career for you."

They all laughed.

"Actually," replied Peter, "you might not need a new career. This reward is one million dollars."

No one was laughing now—they all stared at Peter with their mouths hanging open. When Ginger's knees buckled, Jason and Mace caught her before she hit the floor and place her in a chair. Sage held her mother's hand, trying to reassure her that everything was fine, while Cinnamon fanned her face with a dog-eared copy of *The F.B.I. Field Agent's Manual*, fearing she would pass out from shock.

"A million dollars?" Ginger finally managed to gasp.

"That's what they told me," replied Peter. "You'll receive the paper work in the mail."

"Yeah," quipped Sage, winking at her mother. "There's always a catch."

Mace pressed the elevator button, as they all prepared to leave.

"Good luck with your new job," Peter said to Cinnamon.

"Thanks," she nodded. "Are you off to another secret spy mission?"

"I plan to take some time off—maybe change directions."

Cinnamon raised one curious eyebrow, "Stop by if you're ever in the neighborhood. You know where to find me."

"You can count on it," he said, smiling.

Jason rode down in the elevator with the McCormick family, while the three F.B.I. agents finished packing up their equipment.

As the group exited the elevator, Jason gently touched Sage's elbow. "Would you like to have a cup of coffee with me? I hear they've got *killer* desserts in the restaurant here," he winked.

Sage chuckled at his tacky pun, sensing that it might be time to call a truce in their relationship. "Sure, I'd like that."

She told her family about her change in plans, and Mace gave Ginger's hand a knowing squeeze.

* * * * * * * * * *

The rest of the McCormick family piled into Cinnamon's SUV and headed for their long-awaited journey home. Cinnamon climbed into the driver's seat with Mace beside her, while Ginger, Pepper and Curry collapsed gratefully onto the back seat.

"Thank God that ordeal is over," sighed Pepper. "I can't wait to crawl into bed."

The others nodded in complete agreement.

"So what do you girls plan to buy with your million-dollar reward?" asked Curry.

"It's not just ours," countered Ginger. "The whole family played a part in capturing Gordon Ellis. We all get an equal share."

"Of course," agreed Pepper. "But I'm pretty sure Curry and I know where our share is going." The twin sisters smiled at each other, their eyes glittering with excitement.

"I'll have to think about how I want to spend my part," replied Cinnamon. "If I hadn't just been offered a dream job at a fabulous restaurant, I would consider opening my own place. Maybe later."

"What's that in the road?" asked Mace, as the headlights flashed across a large, brown bag in the center of the narrow two-lane roadway.

Cinnamon squinted, as she brought the Jeep to a stop directly in front of the object. "It looks like a large duffle bag. Maybe it fell off the back of a truck."

"Pull over to the shoulder," said Mace, "and I'll get it off the road."

Cinnamon pulled over and stopped. "Do you need my help?"

"Let me see how heavy it is first."

Mace jumped out of the Jeep and grabbed the large bag. Suddenly it began to move, jerking violently back and forth. Startled, Mace jumped back, as he heard a woman's voice cursing and yelling at the top of her lungs.

The McCormick women stared in stunned silence at the bag flopping around on the roadway, and a terrified Mace jumping around trying to stay out of range. They all bailed out of the Jeep and ran over to help him.

"Get me out of here!" screeched the woman, rolling over and over on the concrete road.

"Hold still," yelled Mace, "so I can help you."

"I'm going to kill that bastard," she shouted. "He did this to me, and I'm going to strangle him with my bare hands!"

Mace began to reassess his original plan. Perhaps it wasn't such a good idea to let this wildcat loose.

"Who are you?" asked Cinnamon, sensing Mace's concern.

"Cinnamon?" asked the woman, "Is that you? I'm Marla Tate. Get me out of here."

"Marla," gasped Cinnamon, clawing desperately at the ropes wrapped tightly around the opening to the bag.

"What the hell are you doing in a bag in the middle of the road?" asked Mace, when they finally managed to release the mightily miffed Marla.

"It was a couple of Clinton's thugs," she snarled. "They grabbed me when I left the hotel, stuffed me into this bag and threw me into the back of a truck. I managed to kick the tailgate open and roll out of the back, but I couldn't get out. I'm going to strangle Clinton for this," she screamed. "Call the Sheriff—call the F.B.I. I was kidnapped and damn near killed! I want those thugs caught and thrown in jail..."

Ginger sighed. Would this nightmare ever end? "Call Peter," she said to Cinnamon.

"I don't know his number," Cinnamon replied.

"Just call 911," suggested Mace.

"No," argued Pepper. "The police will arrive with sirens blaring and we'll be stuck here all night explaining this new development."

"Then call Jason," said Ginger.

"Do you know his number?" asked Cinnamon.

"Give me that phone," demanded Ginger, impatient to get home and stop all this madness. She punched in Sage's cell phone number.

* * * * * * * * * *

At The Grand Hotel, on their way to the restaurant, Jason followed close behind Sage. As they reached the crowded lobby, he placed his hand at the small of her back to guide her through the traffic. Her knees wobbled slightly with his touch.

They were seated, side-by-side, in a semi-circular booth at the back of the restaurant, and asked to see the dessert tray. They practically drooled over the luscious choices, and finally decided on the Black Forest cake—a dense chocolate confection topped with sweet cherries and warm fudge sauce. After the waiter took their food order, there was an awkward moment of silence.

"You know," said Jason, "I've known your family for years, but I never found out why your parents gave all their kids spice names."

Sage smiled. "When my parents met, it was love at first sight and they married soon afterward. Since their names are spices, they didn't want to tempt fate by changing the flow, so they kept the theme going."

"Do you believe in love at first sight?" asked Jason.

Sage stared at the ceiling, then at the floor—anywhere but into his eyes. "I certainly believe in lust at first sight," she said.

Jason leaned closer and whispered into her ear, "There's nothing wrong with a little lust."

His warm breath on her ear and the sound of his deep, sultry voice sent a shiver of excitement down her spine.

Jason put his arm around her shoulders. "Are you cold, Counselor?"

Sage smiled and looked into his warm, brown eyes. "Not anymore."

About the Author

Gloria Hander Lyons began her writing career in 1983, writing craft project articles featured in magazines, such as *Better Homes and Gardens, McCall's, Country Handcrafts* and *Crafts*, with more than 125 articles published.

She then channeled 35 years of training and hands-on experience in the areas of art, interior decorating, crafting and event planning into writing cookbooks and creative how-to books. Her titles cover a wide range of topics including decorating your home, cooking, planning weddings, theme parties and tea parties, crafting and self-publishing, plus humorous slice-of-life stories.

Gloria has had numerous short stories published in *Chicken Soup for the Soul* and several other anthologies. She has also taught interior decorating and self-publishing classes at her local community college.

Always an avid reader, especially of cozy murder mysteries, she couldn't resist writing a mystery of her very own.

Visit her website www.BlueSagePress.com for a list of all her book titles, or her author website: www.GloriaHanderLyons.com to read a few of her sample short stories.

Send questions or comments to:

gloria@bluesagepress.com